SAVAGE FATE

Young Paula Savage was fleeing a tragedy in her past when she came to the little town of Coxbury to be secretary to a wealthy old eccentric. But soon she found how foolish she was to imagine this place would be a haven from horror.

The curse of a crime done long ago shadowed the town with fear, filled it with seething hate. Why had Paula been summoned here? Who was weaving a tightening net of murder around her? And how could she put her fate in the hands of a man she barely knew, no matter how much she needed his protection, and no matter how terrifying her peril grew? . . .

DANGEROUS TO ME

Rae Foley

A DELL BOOK

For Walter and Ann Elliott

Published by
DELL PUBLISHING CO., INC.
1 Dag Hammarskjold Plaza
New York, New York 10017
Copyright © 1959 by Rae Foley
All rights reserved.
No part of this book may be reproduced
in any form without permission in writing
from Dodd, Mead & Company, Inc., New York, New York.

Dell ® TM 681510, Dell Publishing Co., Inc.
Reprinted by arrangement with
Dodd, Mead & Company, Inc.
Printed in the United States of America
First Dell printing—August 1974

One

The passport to murder appeared in the form of a large block display advertisement in the Help Wanted section of *The New York Times*.

> WANTED Young woman who is intelligent, cheerful and long suffering to assist in assembling material for a book on local history. Highbrows need not apply. Self-pitying females must not apply. Dominating dames dare not apply. Box 717X.

It was, she thought, just what she had been looking for, the kind of work any reasonably intelligent, college-bred woman could handle, with no ominous demand for references. If any questions should crop up later, she might be able to sidetrack them. Anyhow, there was no point in borrowing trouble.

When she had written an answer to the advertisement she scrawled in her big angular writing, "Paula—" and then sat staring at the fire escape that blocked what little light filtered through her window on the court. A long time later she added the word "Savage." The ink was paler; the two names didn't quite match.

The answer came a week later in the midst of a New York heat wave. The tiny entrance to the dilapidated brownstone front in which Paula had a furnished one-room apartment was so breathlessly hot that for once she was grateful that the outside door always stood open, a fact that she had battled fruitlessly with the superintendent. The latter had listened and shrugged.

"They forget their keys," she said, "and I'm not going to get up half a dozen times a night to let people in. Anyhow, let's face it. People who live here, dearie, don't have much in the way of valuables lying around. If you expect a doorman for what you pay—well—"

Standing in the dark entrance beside the mailboxes, Paula read the letter, which suggested that she call on hers sincerely, Helen Quarles, on Thursday at five to discuss the local history. The address was a modest and conventional women's hotel in midtown Manhattan. The wording of the advertisement suggested an eccentric man, that of the letter a conventional woman. The address destroyed any hope she might have had that there would be enough money for a decent salary.

At any rate, it would be some sort of salary and the only other mail in her box was a tart reminder that she had not paid her garage bill. The Dodge, she decided must be added to the things she had to learn to do without, though it was all she had left that Derek had given her. Derek—from long practice she switched her mind away from him.

When she had kept the appointment at five that Thursday she went through a gloomy lobby filled with querulous elderly women and was directed to room 4H, which was through a fire door and beside a freight elevator. A woman who seemed like a black shadow against the light was waiting for her.

"Miss Savage? I am Helen Quarles. Do come in. How kind of you to venture out on such a hot day. Perhaps this chair—"

Borne along on a flood of little agitated exclamations, Paula found herself being pushed into the only armchair the room boasted. A single bed, a chest of drawers, and a small desk with a straight chair filled the space so that when the two women were seated they were almost knee to knee. A noisy electric fan stirred the air without cooling it, fighting a losing battle with the afternoon sun that beat relentlessly on the window.

Miss Quarles was in her middle sixties, a dowdy woman but exquisitely neat. Through her nervous spate of words, her chirping social manner, the chief impression she gave was that of tension, evidenced by the cords in her neck, the frown that furrowed her forehead, the too-intent expression of her eyes. A neurotic, Paula realized, her heart sinking, only half listening to the older woman's babble of words.

". . . hate to ask any woman to come to see me alone in New York, though this hotel is so safe, so protected. . . I'm afraid to go out by myself in the city. But perhaps it doesn't frighten you so much. How lovely it is to be young!"

Paula smiled vaguely. Ten minutes, she thought. She would stay ten minutes.

"Well, my dear," Miss Quarles said with a self-conscious titter, "I suppose we must 'get down to business.' " She seemed to put the words in quotation marks as an indication of their delicate humor. "I sent all the answers to the ad—and you'd be surprised how many there were —such a peculiar way of phrasing it—straight to Mr. Morison. He selected three possible—candidates, I suppose we can call them."

Again she tittered nervously, though her face never lost its look of strain. "I saw the other two today but they weren't quite—well, not to be snobbish, I didn't think they would fit in—but the moment I saw you—"

"Mr. Morison?" Paula asked, trying to drive the nervous spate of words into a channel.

"My—principal, I suppose you would call him. We are old friends but I am acting for him purely in a business capacity. He relies so completely on my judgment, you see."

Paula saw vividly. The genteel poor; the unequipped woman who lived from hand to mouth, being helped in the only way she would accept help, by the pretense of services paid for.

She nodded, accepting the fiction. "Then Mr. Morison is not here today?"

"Oh, my dear, he never comes to New York any more. He is almost crippled with arthritis. Such a pity, for he has always been an active man. That's why he decided to take up this little project—to occupy his mind." She managed to make it sound like busy work for pre-school children.

"What is the project, Miss Quarles?"

"A history of the village where he has lived all his life. So absurd, my dear! There never were more than five hundred people and since the flood it is really a deserted village. But Ed has his heart set on it. A microcosm of our civilization, he calls it.

"Actually, I think he needs someone to keep him working. You'd be living at his house, of course, and no expenses of any kind. And," she took a long breath, "ninety dollars a week. Really, the salaries they pay these days! I had no idea. My own little income has gone down and down."

Out of New York and the heat of summer, Paula thought jubilantly, and all expenses paid. I can put the salary away and build a backlog.

Before she could speak, Miss Quarles plunged on heavily. "Mr. Morison liked your letter much the best. If that arrangement doesn't appeal to you, I was to go up to $115 in your case."

"You speak all your part at once, cues and all," Paula thought in amusement.

"A hundred and fifteen would be all right," she said firmly, remembering the garage bill. "When would Mr. Morison like me to start? That is, of course, if you are satisfied."

"Oh, at once. As soon as possible. He is in a lot of pain and he needs something to take his mind off it."

"I haven't even asked where Mr. Morison lives."

"How stupid of me! He is in Connecticut. A village called Coxbury." Miss Quarles searched Paula's face as though expecting some reaction. When there was none she seemed to relax.

"What is it like?" Paula asked idly.

"It used to be lovely, idyllic, you might say. But that was before—" Miss Quarles got up to adjust the fan. "Before the flood," she finished, but Paula was sure that was not what she had started to say. "I don't know what it is like now. I've lived abroad so long. I haven't been in America for twenty years. I don't even know a soul except the people in Coxbury. I never expected to come back. But what can I do?"

She made a bewildered gesture. "Stocks are such queer things. My money was most carefully invested and yet it has just—dwindled. There is nothing left but $250 a month and my little cottage in Coxbury. Every year Ed used to rent it for me but—there were complaints. I don't understand why; it's a nice cottage. Somehow, word got around and no one will take it any more, so I have to live in it."

"You don't," Paula commented, "seem to care much about Coxbury."

"I'm afraid," Miss Quarles said. "I'm afraid to go back. Didn't you see it in the paper? Lenny Horgan was released today."

Paula looked at her blankly. Lenny Horgan? The name was familiar in the dim way of one seen in print. A name from the past. A name and a picture. The picture of a good-looking boy with dark hair and eyes that glinted from under drooping lids as though they were too lazy to hold them open; and a half-mocking, half-defiant smile. Of course! The notorious boy murderer of twenty years ago whose story had been rehashed recently in the press since word had come that he was to be pardoned.

"But what on earth," she asked, "has Lenny Horgan to do—"

"His mother lives in Coxbury. He's going there." Miss Quarles's voice grew shrill. "He'd never have been released while his stepfather lived. Forrest Bulow fought any attempt to get him a pardon. But as soon as Forrest died, Lenny's mother determined to have him freed. Claire, Forrest's own daughter, wrote me about it. She was frantic. She knew Lenny through and through. She realized Sylvia had no right to set him loose on the world."

"But he can't be dangerous, you know." Paula was aware of the strained impatience in her voice.

Miss Quarles's eyes held hers with a glitter that was repellent. "He is dangerous to me," she said.

Paula wished heartily that she were anywhere else. This woman was not neurotic, she was psychotic. Why it's true, the girl thought in surprise, you can actually smell fear.

"He hates me," the older woman said. "He has never forgiven me. I tell you, I know. I've been warned often enough. You are too young to remember the case. What are you—twenty-three?"

"Twenty-nine."

"Really?" Miss Quarles was as easily distracted as a kitten. "You seem younger. So triumphantly young. Perhaps it is being beautiful that gives you such an undefeated look."

Bitterness welled up in Paula's throat in a hot steam, but for the first time in months pity for someone else was stronger than pity for herself, though she thought: Triumphant! Undefeated! Dear God!

"Anyhow, you wouldn't remember, but it was a sensational case at the time. For once, Coxbury was famous." A look of alarm crossed Miss Quarles's face. "But surely Ed Morison wouldn't dream of putting the Horgan murder trial in his book, would he? He couldn't do that to Lenny's mother. He has been in love with Sylvia for thirty years."

She got up a little blindly and shifted the fan again. "You had better know. If you are going to Coxbury, you had better know."

Paula started to say, "I'm not going to Coxbury." Then she remembered $115 a week plus expenses and cool nights in Connecticut. After all, she need not see Miss Quarles nor the cottage in which no one wanted to live.

"You see," Miss Quarles said jerkily, "I found the body. I saw Lenny run out of the theater after he killed her. I was the only witness. It was my evidence that led to his arrest and my testimony that got him sent up for life. They didn't execute him because he was only sixteen. Though you are just as dead if you are killed by someone sixteen as by someone sixty. They should—"

"An eye for an eye?"

To Paula's surprise, Miss Quarles winced as though she had been struck.

"My dear, you are right, of course. An eye for an eye. Revenge, really. It wouldn't bring Evelyn back, even if—" She caught her breath and was silent.

Even if we wanted her back. She might as well have screamed it.

"Was Evelyn—?"

"Evelyn Dwight. Her mother was a school friend of mine who went to South America with her husband. A business trip. She left Evelyn with me. She thought she'd be safe." Miss Quarles stopped to steady her voice and patted her damp face delicately with her handkerchief.

"I had moved to Coxbury and bought my little cottage there to be near Sylvia. She was the dearest friend I had in the world. And so beautiful. As placid as a mountain lake. All still surface and bright reflections. She was Sylvia Horgan then, a widow with one son, Lenny.

"Well, she married Forrest Bulow. I never understood it. Of course, he was a wealthy widower and Sylvia was poor but I never thought money mattered to her. Forrest was terribly possessive and a—violent man. Once he shot a dog of his because it kept running away to the people next door. It was his, you see, and he couldn't stand to have it prefer anyone else. A frightening man, I always thought. Well, Forrest had two children of his own, Claire and Willis. Even as a child Claire had a lot of character, like her father, but I never thought Willis amounted to much. He was one of those secretive, repressed boys. So unnatural, I always say. It used to make Forrest furious that Lenny was so much smarter than his own son and Willis knew how his father felt. It just seemed to make him draw deeper into himself.

"But Sylvia's own boy Lenny was a bright child. A chess prodigy. That's what caused all the publicity at the time of the murder. He had just won some sort of international championship, and there were stories about him in the press, his picture on the cover of a weekly magazine and interviews on radio programs. A ridiculous amount of fuss over a sixteen-year-old boy.

"Well, everything went fine until that day in August. It had been the gayest season. Something doing every minute. The three children at the Bulows, and a nice local boy named Stanley Tooling, who has married Claire since then. Evelyn Dwight was with me and Ed Morison had his nephew, Ross Bentwick. I don't see how I came to put Ross last. He was always the ringleader of everything. Ed had such high hopes for him. He was devoted to the boy but, from what I can make out, Ross has been a bitter disappointment. Bitter."

Paula looked up with sharpened interest. "Not Ross Bentwick the actor?"

"Do you know him?"

"I have seen him act. Several times, in fact. I remember him particularly as the guilty doctor in *The Poisoner* and as Richard the Third. I've never experienced such a powerful sense of evil."

"I don't see why Ross needs a profession, particularly one in which he makes such an exhibition of himself. He's going to have all Ed's money." Miss Quarles added, startled, "That is, if Ed leaves him his money.

"Well, anyhow, it had been a nice summer. But even then I had a feeling—of course, I was responsible for Evelyn and I wasn't used to children. I didn't know how much supervision they should have and I couldn't always tell—Evelyn was such a liar. I think the only time she ever told me the truth was the day before she was killed. I found her putting that stone back into place. The way she did it I knew she was hiding something. I let her know I had a pretty good idea what had been going on at the shack and it had to stop.

"It's funny, Miss Savage. A childless old maid like me gets queer ideas about children. I thought they were like those pretty pictures in women's magazines. It's a shock to know what a child's mind can be. Sometimes when I look back I think Lenny—I think perhaps—"

Her face crumpled and tears rolled down her cheeks. "His mother was my dearest friend and I destroyed her son. You don't know what it is to live with the fact that you've destroyed a man's life."

Paula's cup dropped from numb fingers and splashed over the carpet. "I'm terribly sorry. I don't know what made me so clumsy."

"It doesn't matter. How white you are, my dear! I'm ashamed of myself. Dragging out that gloomy old story But I thought you had better be prepared, and I had to talk about it. For twenty years it has haunted me. Why did Lenny kill her? Why? If I only knew who put him up to it. If I could only be sure—but I wasn't sure." Her hands gripped each other. "Not sure enough to say anything in court.

"Well, it's too late now, in any case, and it might not have made as much difference as I've sometimes feared. Anyhow, we'll be businesslike, shall we? I'll call Ed while you are here so we can have it all settled and no mistake."

She put through a collect call for Coxbury. "Ed? . . . I've found just the one . . . Yes, Paula Savage . . . I know you liked her best but to be on the safe side, to earn the fee you so generously . . . Tomorrow?"

She broke off to ask Paula, "Can you be ready tomorrow?"

Paula nodded. "If you aren't afraid of a battered old car, I'll drive you up."

"Fine. We're," Miss Quarles's voice rose over a sudden racket in the corridor outside, "driving up. Would you ask Joe to open my cottage, have the water . . . Thank you, Ed."

She wrote Paula's name, address and telephone number on a slip of paper and tucked it into a zippered compartment in a bulging handbag. "I always keep notes there. I always have. Then I can find them."

She took Paula to the door and the latter arranged to meet her at eleven the next morning.

Paula found her way blocked by deliverymen who

were maneuvering a large couch into the freight elevator. She pressed back against the door to give them more space and heard the telephone ring in the room behind her.

Miss Quarles said, "Hello." After a long silence she spoke again and the voice was quite different from the one Paula had been hearing for the past hour.

"Yes, I'm going back, but it's all right now . . . I'm not afraid any more . . . I've been telling the whole thing . . . You wouldn't know her . . . Paula Savage, Ed Morison's new assistant and a highly intelligent young woman, though you wouldn't think it at first because she's so pretty . . . Just in case anything happened to me. I wanted someone to know . . . Well, I'd prefer to call it life insurance."

Two

As the big car emerged from the prison gates onto the main road, the man at the wheel put his foot down on the accelerator.

"We've done it," he called exultantly to the two silent people on the back seat. "Lenny! God, it's wonderful, it's —Lenny!"

"Thanks to you, Stan. Where are you taking me?" There was no resonance in the voice, only a kind of passive acceptance.

"New York. A friend of your mother's has lent her an apartment for the night. It's all right. We've got permission to take you out of the state for twenty-four hours to duck the reporters."

"You're going to have a job doing that. They are right on our heels."

Stan Tooling laughed. "Not for long," he said confidently. "Willis is going to run interference. At that narrow turn a couple of miles farther on, he's going to park right across the road and hold them until we are far enough ahead to lose them. You'll have a night of peace and tomorrow we are all going up to Coxbury."

A few minutes later he took a curve fast. He touched his horn and another car, moving across the road behind him, closed it completely.

"See?" Stan called. "Good old Willis! He'll hold them for us." The silence in the back of the car disturbed him and his round cheerful face was clouded. "Sylvia, darling," he said, "isn't it marvelous?"

She responded to his appeal. Poor Stan, the perennial Old Grad, was trying to turn Lenny's release from prison into a kind of college reunion, to whip up a synthetic mood of celebration.

"Marvelous," she agreed, "but we need a little time to get adjusted, my dear."

"Sure," he said awkwardly. "Sure."

Sylvia Horgan Bulow looked anxiously at her son. How he had changed! So far she had found almost nothing she recognized in him. The charming boy of twenty years ago had given place to a stout, middle-aged man with a balding head; steel-rimmed glasses covered the eyes that had been so mocking and were now so questioning, so diffident. How were they to put away the past, wipe it out, and start again? O God, she thought in despair, have I done this to my son?

Nothing seemed to have survived the past without change except for the unswerving friendship of her stepson Willis, who was blocking the road behind them, and of Stanley Tooling, who was driving her son back to normal life. In spite of his marriage to her stepdaughter Claire, who hated Lenny, he was standing now, as he had from the beginning, firm as a rock beside Lenny.

Sylvia Bulow took off her hat and dropped it on the seat beside her. Her hair was still the same, Lenny thought with a shock of recognition. Still glistening black, with only a touch of gray. And her wonderful eyes. But otherwise—how could life be so cruel, do this grotesque thing to his beautiful mother? If she had just faded out, as most women do, it wouldn't matter so much. But she had become monstrously fat. He could not bear to look at her and yet he kept doing it; quick, almost sly glances, seeking some trace of her former beauty.

"Lenny," she said abruptly, "Helen Quarles is going to be there in Coxbury. Ed Morison told me. She didn't want to go but she can't rent the cottage any more and she has to live in it. She came back from Europe in May and she's staying at that women's hotel she always used to talk about." Sylvia repeated apologetically, "She didn't want to go."

Lenny wrested his attention from the fascinating scenes he was watching from the car window, the incredible changes that had taken place. "But why shouldn't she go back?" When there was no answer he asked in a curious tone, "Is it because she testified against me? Is she afraid of me?"

"Lenny!"

Something discordant in his laugh disturbed her. Perhaps it was because it was the first time she had heard him laugh.

Stan threaded his way expertly through the New York traffic and drew up outside a middle-priced apartment building on the West Side. No, thanks, he wouldn't come in. He'd see them in Coxbury tomorrow. He drove off with a wave of the hand, festive and jubilant to the last.

As Sylvia turned to enter the lobby, her son hesitated. "Is it all right—that is, am I free to go out?"

"Of course," she told him.

"Then, if you don't mind, I'd like to take a walk. By myself. It's been a long time. Don't wait up for me."

Sylvia opened her lips to protest and saw his expression. "Go ahead," she told him. "Have fun."

II

LENNY HORGAN RELEASED. Stan Tooling let the paper drop onto the floor beside his easy chair, one of those heart-rest deals Claire had insisted on his using, though his heart was as sound as a bell. At the moment it was also singularly at peace, as it had been ever since the moment when he had driven out of the prison gates.

He pushed on the arms and the chair slid back so that he reclined almost as though he were lying down. He raised his tall glass of planter's punch and drank. It had never before tasted so good. Perhaps that was because of the hot night, though since Claire had installed air conditioning, the smart little townhouse in the east sixties was pleasantly cool. Claire, he thought with pride, was the most efficient woman he knew. He would never have been as happy with anyone else, in spite of the fact they were so different. Or perhaps because of it.

No one, as he was well aware, had ever believed the

marriage would last, let alone that they would make a terrific success of it. Claire, like her old man, had a driving ambition, though she wasn't violent about it, and he —well, Stan supposed easygoing was the word for him. But they seemed to balance each other.

He took another sip of the planter's punch. Suddenly he knew why it tasted so good. He had never before felt that he had a right to enjoy it. Not while Lenny was in prison, unable to enjoy anything. Well, that was done. After twenty years, he and Sylvia and Willis had turned the trick and there were the headlines and the pictures to prove it.

Claire was sore, of course. She had always resented Lenny, just as she had resented Sylvia. People seemed to get that way about stepmothers. Claire was going to be difficult. He must be careful not to make too much of Lenny. Claire might just possibly put her foot down and do or say something that would queer Lenny in Coxbury, so he couldn't get back at all. Stan knew his wife when that lantern jaw of hers set. Nothing would budge her then.

He got up as she came into the room, smiling at her. She was wearing a new white outfit that made the most of her pretty figure, and a new white hat. She looked very smart, he thought proudly. Claire was the best-turned-out woman he knew. Everything Elizabeth Arden's salon could do had been done for her hair and her skin. In most ways she looked much younger than her thirty-eight years. Few people guessed that she was older than he. If it weren't for her jaw she'd be damned good looking. Not that he cared. He'd seen the squares who had to have pretty women to build their egos. But it mattered to Claire. She had always been bitterly jealous of pretty women; even of her stepmother, though Sylvia was so fat now there was no trace of her great beauty.

"You look very bonnie," he said. "I like you in white."

Claire returned his smile and came across the room to kiss him, though even then her eyes were darting around, checking on her possessions to make sure they were all present and accounted for.

She returned his kiss with an ardor that would have surprised even those who knew her well, and then drew away from his arms to bend over and pick up the newspaper he had dropped. Before putting it in the magazine rack she glanced at the front page and the happiness went out of her face.

"Well," she said, "I hope you are satisfied."

Stan recognized the tone. She was building up to a quarrel.

"I'll fix you a planter's punch," he said. "Just what the doctor ordered on a night like this."

"John can do it."

"There's nothing John can do I can't do better," Stan said complacently. "Anyhow, I like it this way. The servants upstairs and us by ourselves. For once, the phone hasn't even rung."

"I shut off the phone so it couldn't ring. The reporters telephoned all day."

"The repor—oh, I see."

"Well, what can you expect?" When Stan discreetly made no answer she insisted, "This is what you wanted. Isn't it?"

She was going to go through with her quarrel, and no stopping her. Better let her get it out of her system.

"Yes," he told her evenly, "this is what I wanted. Lenny got a raw deal."

"A raw deal! He never was any good. That wasn't the first time he had been in trouble. It was just the worst. He had stolen money from Dad. He'd stolen cars. He—"

"Any kid wants pocket money and your father was always hard on him, Claire. Your father was a hard man. And unforgiving. He was as strong on punishment as the boys in the Old Testament. He'd have thrown you or Willis out and let you starve if he had caught you disobeying him. And let's be honest about it. He resented the fact that Lenny was so much brighter than his own son."

"Well, God knows, Willis didn't mind," Claire snapped. "If he is my own brother, I'll have to admit he has no more spirit than a sponge."

"Your father did that, too," Stan said bluntly. "He destroyed all the gumption Willis had. The poor kid was scared of him."

"Oh, nonsense. I was never afraid of Dad."

"Weren't you?" he asked.

"And you weren't, Stan. You know that."

"Well, he wasn't my father. And he was always nice to me."

"I'm glad you admit that."

"I've always admitted it, dear. He took a fancy to me and built me up in his business. I'd never have got this far on my own." He looked around the beautifully appointed living room. "Only—"

"Well?"

"Only," Stan said slowly, "he didn't really do it for me; he did it because I wasn't Willis—or Lenny."

Claire laughed impatiently. She laid her hand on his shoulder and he put his hand on top of it. Claire needed a lot of reassurance, at least where affection was concerned.

"The trouble with you," she said, "is that you can't just accept things when they are done for you. You've always felt guilty because Dad did more for you than he did for Willis."

"And Lenny."

She pulled away her hand. "Oh, stop it! Lenny's no good. He never was any good. What should they have done? Given him a medal? You seem to forget he killed Evelyn."

"Oh, yes," Stan said wearily, "he killed her. But who wouldn't have killed her if they could have got away with it?"

"Stan!"

"She knew about you and me. You hated her yourself, Claire."

She had stretched out her hand. For a moment the

red-tipped fingers were motionless, then they reached for a cigarette and lit it. "You'd like me to admit that I'm glad Evelyn is dead, wouldn't you? So I'm glad!"

"Sorry, darling. Let's forget it. It's over now."

"Over! For Lenny, maybe. But it's just starting for us. Can you imagine what Coxbury is going to be like, with Lenny living at Willis's house just because Sylvia wants to be there? I can't help but feel sorry for Ivy. Just sick."

"After all," Stan pointed out, "Lenny might be coming to our house. Your father left it to your stepmother. It was darned generous of Sylvia to turn it over to you."

"That was her way of getting back at Dad," Claire said shrewdly, "even if he never knew it. He built it for her, so she gave it away. Anyhow, she always liked Willis better than she did me. What burns me up is that Willis's wife is the one who has to suffer by having Lenny as a house guest."

"Ivy is a nice person. She'll be all right about it."

"Of course, she's nice. That's the trouble. Junior League and Social Register and all that. For a girl with her background—"

"I know I haven't any background. I'm just the guy from across the tracks."

"Oh, Stan, I didn't mean that!"

"What did you mean?"

"I—oh, hell! There's no use talking. No, I don't want a drink. I have a raging headache. I'm going to bed. Don't disturb me tonight, will you?"

"Best thing you could do. I'll be in the study if you want me. I have some paper work to finish up tonight so I'll be clear for the summer. I'll see you in the morning."

"Don't work too late."

"I won't." He kissed her, held her tight for a moment and then let her go.

III

When there was no answer to his ring, Willis Bulow groped for his door key and let himself into the big duplex apartment on Fifth Avenue. He was a slender man, with small neat features and impeccable grooming, as though he relied more on his tailor's efforts than on his own to give him distinction.

His first impression was that the apartment was deserted and he had a sinking feeling in his stomach. Suppose, after all, Ivy had gone. From the beginning there had been a lurking fear that some day he would come home and find her gone.

There was no sound of movement, no sign of the butler or the parlor maid. After waiting a moment, Willis dropped his hat on a chair in the big foyer and went quickly through the lower floor of the apartment. A long drawing room ran across most of the front of the building, facing Central Park, and because of the heat the draperies had not been drawn. He could see lights in the buildings on Central Park West and on the great blinking signs at Columbus Circle.

Willis stared at them as though trying to hold off the inevitable moment when he would have to face his loss. Then he went swiftly from room to room, searching the small morning room, the library, the great dining room, the kitchen and pantries. No one.

He ran up the pretty circular staircase in the drawing room to the floor above and stopped short, his heart thudding. There was a light under Ivy's bedroom door! He tapped softly.

"Willis?" she called. "Come in, dear."

He went inside and stood leaning against the door frame, his legs weak from reaction. His wife came out of her dressing room in a long green velvet housecoat that swirled around her feet. Ivy's clothes were always dramatic. Her hair, like a soft black cloud, was combed in a pompadour above her vivid narrow face. Her green eyes were shining.

"Just out of the tub, darling. I was so hot and sticky, though this apartment is heavenly cool. Just the same, it will be wonderful to get up to Connecticut tomorrow. How ghastly you look! This awful heat wave."

He was tempted to break through the barrier, to say, "I couldn't find you; I was afraid you had left me." But the bars of his long-imposed restraint were too strong for him.

"Where is everyone?" he asked. He spoke with an unconvincing British accent. Everything about Willis was slightly unconvincing.

"Mamie is getting married."

"Mamie?"

"Brown's daughter."

"Brown?"

"The butler, Willis! Brown. You're wool-gathering. We gave the servants the evening off so they could go to Mamie's wedding. Surely you remember. The day you gave Brown the check for Mamie's wedding present."

"Oh, of course. It slipped my mind."

"Do sit down. You look as though you were ready to drop. Did you and Stan have any difficulty at the prison?"

"No, it went smoothly. The reporters were there in force but Stan got away to a fast start and then I blocked the road when he passed me."

Willis looked around Ivy's room—how long it had been since he had entered it—and sat uneasily on a small green-satin chair, feeling like an intruder. Ivy flung herself onto the chaise longue, the housecoat falling open. There was nothing under it. She drew it together very slowly. How enchanting she was! Not pretty, perhaps, but gay and delightful. He wondered if she ever thought how long it was since they had made love. He couldn't read much in her face. Just the question that had been there for a long time.

"Ivy, are you sure it's going to be all right? That it won't be too tough for you?"

"You mean having your stepbrother—having Lenny—in the house?"

"Yes."

"But I've told you before, Willis! Over and over. I don't mind at all. I knew about him when we were married. I think his mother is a darling. You're fond of them both. I don't mind his being with us."

There might as well be a sound barrier between them, she thought in discouragement. The eager warmth and reassurance in her voice did not reach him at all.

"Helen Quarles is going back to Coxbury," he said dully. "She was the key witness in Lenny's trial. She—there will be trouble. I feel it."

"She's the woman the girl lived with, isn't she? The girl Lenny killed? What was she like, Willis?"

He was silent a long time. "She—well, Evelyn was awfully pretty. A blonde. She looked a young fifteen but she was seventeen. A very mature seventeen."

"She'd been around, I gather."

Willis's face turned a dark red and then the color drained out, leaving it white. "She was vile," he said, and heard his own voice. He cleared his throat. "But I must warn you that with Lenny and Helen Quarles both going back, there is bound to be talk in a village like Coxbury."

"Of course there will be talk," she said in her quick, eager voice. "Hard words break no bones, as my nurse used to tell me. Don't be so afraid of what people think or say. After all, most of them are perfectly well meaning. They are just interested and it's a nugget of news. A nice juicy nugget. You can't blame them."

"I don't blame them."

"I know," she said. "You never blame anyone but yourself."

"Oh, I don't—"

"Yes, you do." Ivy sat up. "All your life you've let people abuse you and you've felt guilty because you were yourself and not what they wanted you to be." As he started to protest she flung out her hand. "No, listen! You've helped Lenny get free. Good! Now get yourself out of prison."

He was silent. Behind the dark glasses he had recently taken to wearing she could not see his eyes.

"So far as I am concerned," she went on, "I thought Forrest Bulow was a prize stinker, even if he was your father. He was a brutal man, a ruthless man. The way

he kept you under his thumb, making you act as his secretary and building up Stan Tooling in the business. And
not just because Stan married Claire. It was long before
Stan became his son-in-law."

"Stan's a good guy and better at the job than I'd ever
have been," Willis said. "I never liked the business."

Ivy Bulow watched her husband with a mingling of ex-
asperation and tenderness. If he would assert himself just
once! How could children of the same parents be as unlike as Willis and Claire?

"You are free now," she told him. "What are you going to do with your freedom, Willis?"

"I don't know."

"But surely—" She got up with one of her quick move-
ments and walked across the room in a swirl of velvet.
"Surely there is something you'd like better than anything else." She laughed and snapped her fingers at him.
"Quick! Answer before you start to think."

"Working with boys," he surprised himself by saying.
"Delinquents. Or kids who might become delinquents."

The light faded out of her face. "You aren't even trying to get out of your private prison," she cried. "You
have your own life to live and you haven't begun yet.
Those delinquents—they aren't your problem."

"Aren't they?"

"Just because Lenny—"

"At least," he told her, "Lenny has paid his debt. In
some ways I almost envy him."

IV

"Hot enough for you?" the man at the kiosk said as he
handed Ross Bentwick his usual paper, neatly folded so
he could tuck it under his arm. "Ninety-eight out here at
four o'clock." He added with a kind of gloomy satisfaction, "In the shade."

He took another look at his customer. Sure is beat, he
thought. If he's not a candidate for the A.A. I never saw
one. Some night he'll see things crawling out of the walls

and they'll haul him off to Bellevue.

Ross nodded to him, turned into the entrance of the Ninth Street apartment building where he lived and walked down the hall to the back. He let himself in, flung open the windows before he stripped off his coat. It had been a charming apartment, with a white fireplace and bookshelves on either side to the ceiling, and French doors opening out on a garden in back. Right now, it was run to seed, with clothes scattered around, dirty glasses strewn everywhere, and the furniture undusted. A pigsty, he thought sourly. But what the hell?

When he stepped out of the cold shower, he toweled his hair dry, put on a pair of shorts and padded into the kitchenette in bare feet. He poured himself a stiff hooker of straight gin which he swallowed in two gulps and made a face. Then he jabbed open a can of cold beer for a chaser.

Back in the living room he abandoned a big easy chair because it made him too warm and pulled a straight chair near the window. God, it was hot! He drank out of the can that was beaded with moisture, set it on the window sill and opened the paper.

LENNY HORGAN RELEASED. There was a large picture with a smaller oval insert of a blond girl with wide blue eyes and a knowing smile. "You little bitch," he said softly.

He studied the bigger picture. So that was what twenty years in prison had made of Lenny. For a long time Ross brooded over the two pictures. On impulse, he went into the bathroom and looked at his own face in the shaving mirror, studying with detachment the bloodshot eyes, the pouches under them, the deeply etched lines. "If you don't look like the end of a misspent life," he told himself, "I don't know who does."

Twenty years. He tried to push out of his mind the succession of days that made up twenty years. A man's youth. All his youth. And for what? For easing Evelyn Dwight out of life. God damn her to hell! What foul luck that Helen Quarles had chosen that night to go to the movies and had happened to sit right behind them. Happened? She had probably followed them. She must have known—have guessed—

Automatically he began to dress. He chose a thin, beautifully cut white linen suit and a charcoal shirt. The man of distinction, he mocked himself, finished the beer, tilting his head back until the last drop had gurgled into his mouth, and then went out of the apartment like a man in flight.

It was nearly morning when he returned. As he let himself in, the telephone began to ring. He picked it up, staggering against the desk.

"Wrong number," he snarled.

"Mr. Ross Bentwick?" said the impersonal voice. "Western Union. We have a message for you. Are you ready? 'Please return Coxbury at once. Urgent. If broke you can get ride with Helen Quarles. Call her at that female hostelry in the morning. Uncle Ed.'"

Ross put down the telephone and stumbled into the kitchenette to get a drink. The glass fell out of his hand and shattered in the sink. He began to laugh.

Three

"You don't know what it is to live with the fact that you've destroyed a man's life."

The words accompanied Paula Savage like a drum beat, followed her down the hot street and into the subway, where a blast of stale air struck her when the door opened. She pushed her way in, caught at a strap—sometimes it helped to be tall—where she swayed now against a heavy overheated woman on the left, now against a coatless man on the right, whose newspaper threatened her eyes.

Over his shoulder she looked at the headline: LENNY HORGAN RELEASED. She saw the man who seemed to stand at bay, encircled by avid newsmen. Why couldn't they let him alone? At least, he had paid for what he had done, which was more than most people did.

Instead of Lenny Horgan, she saw Derek looking out at her from the newsprint, saw the expression of incredulity that faded and left his face blank, saw the bright stain that spread over his white shirt.

She wasn't going to live it over again. She wasn't. But she did, of course. She remembered trying in vain to open the door. Derek had pocketed the key.

"There's only one way you'll ever leave me," Derek said. "Only one way. You know that, don't you?"

The dark rage faded and he was clinging to her, imploring her, and that was worse, in a way. Then, when she couldn't bear it any longer, there was the revolver and the sharp explosion and Derek with that look of shocked disbelief.

The man in front got up and pressed her down into his seat. "You all right, Lady? Better put your head down. Way down."

She looked up into the anxious, workworn face of an elderly man.

"Thanks. I'm all right. Just the heat," she said.

"Sure is a scorcher. After the spring we've had I guess no one believed it would ever warm up like this."

She smiled her thanks and pushed her way off at the Cathedral Parkway station.

Before going upstairs, she stopped at the superintendent's slatternly apartment at the rear of the first floor to notify her that she was leaving in the morning.

"You mightta give me notice. I coulda rented it yesterday. Now it'll stand empty God knows how long. I won't be here and I wouldn't trust my sister's judgment. She'll be in charge while I get a week's vacation at Atlantic City. Sadie means well but she'd take in anyone. Oh, well, can't be helped, I guess."

Tonight, Paula didn't mind the heat. She stripped off everything but panties and bra while she packed. Tomorrow, she'd be out of New York. In Connecticut, the nights would be cool.

When everything was done, she locked the door, though a child, she thought, could have picked the flimsy lock, and went to bed. For weeks she had slept badly but tonight, with a decision made, with some sort of plan for the future, she slept deeply.

She sat bolt upright in bed, her heart thumping. A shot had been fired beside her bed. She had heard it, had seen the flash. Then she saw the jagged light at her window, followed by a roll of thunder. An electric storm. That's all it was. An electric storm.

She propped herself up on her elbow, listening to the growl and reverberations of thunder, watching the lightning flash continuously. She wasn't afraid. Not exactly afraid. But it was a noisy storm and very close. The flashes of lightning and the sound of thunder seemed to synchronize. There was nothing to worry about. The high buildings acted as lightning conductors for the little ones. Someone had told her that. But no one could sleep in such a racket.

She hadn't put on a nightgown. It was too hot. Now some queer feeling made her draw the sheet over her naked body. As though someone were looking at her, which was ridiculous. She discovered that she was straining to hear, listening not to the uproar of the thunder storm but for sounds within the room. Lightning flashes illuminated parts of it fleetingly. No one was there. No one could be there.

A wind was rising and the curtains blew in, bringing a spatter of rain with them. Then they blew out. There was a draft from somewhere. She saw a dim light reflected on the wall and sat up abruptly, swinging her long slender legs onto the floor, groping for slippers. That was the hall light. Her door was wide open.

She went over to close it, saw the key in the lock outside the door. Half a dozen keys hung from the ring. She jerked out the key, closed the door and braced a chair under the knob. She switched on the light and looked in the bathroom, in the closet and, feeling rather foolish, under the bed. Of course, there was nothing—there was nobody in the room. Whoever had tried to get in her room and succeeded in unlocking the door must have been startled when the thunder awakened her. He had run without waiting to collect the keys.

She started to turn out the light and hesitated. Like most women she felt unsafe in the dark. She left the light burning and went back to bed, propped up on her pillows, watching the door, listening. It was nearly morning before she slept.

The morning was hotter than ever. There was a haze over the sky and steam rose from the sidewalk. Paula sat up groggily, puzzled to find her light was still burning. Then she noticed the chair propped under the door knob and remembered her terror of the night before.

She got out of bed, turned out the light and picked up the key ring from her dresser. She examined it curiously. She ought to report it to the police, she supposed, but it might delay her in leaving for Coxbury. Anyhow, the police—her mind refused to follow the thought through.

She'd tell the superintendent. After all, it was not her own personal responsibility.

What puzzled her was that anyone would bother to burgle a house like this. The tenants were unlikely to have anything of value.

When she had dressed, she opened the door for the expressman who had come for her luggage and went downstairs to give the burglar's keys to the superintendent.

The door was opened by a woman as dirty as the superintendent but even more stupid.

"My sister's gone to Atlantic City for a week . . . Someone tried to break in? . . . Well, I don't say it couldn't happen but the only one who ever complained was old Miss Morris who was always sure there was a man in her room or following her on the street, and she was eighty if she was a day . . . Left those keys in the lock? . . . Well, now, I don't like to take the responsibility of calling in the police while my sister's away. And if nothing's been took . . ."

Paula was curiously relieved when she came out on the street. It was silly to bother the police about trivial matters. She had plenty of time. She decided to take a bus and get a little breeze, even if it was hot. This morning she couldn't endure the thought of a subway.

She walked quickly, the click of her high heels sounding loud on the sidewalk in one of those rare intervals of sudden quiet when traffic is light. And it seemed to her that other feet were keeping step with her. She slowed down and the other footsteps slowed. She increased her pace and the feet that followed her moved more quickly.

Like old Miss Morris, she thought. I'm like old Miss Morris. I imagine men in my room and people following me on the street. She stopped and turned around. There were half a dozen people behind her: a man who had paused to light a cigarette, his face concealed by his hat brim and his cupped hands; a woman who had bent over to tie the lace of an oxford, her face hidden as she bowed her head; a couple of men who gesticulated as they talked and who passed without glancing at her; a girl who went into a cleaning establishment with some dresses over her arm; a boy with a box of flowers.

Paula went on toward the bus stop. Three or four people were waiting and she joined them, surprised to observe how relieved she was to be part of a group. Any group. As though they afforded some sort of protection. It's about time you got out in the country and pulled yourself together, she thought.

The lights turned and the bus lumbered toward them. A taxi careened around it and raced toward the corner where an impatient man, after a glance at his watch, had hailed it. A sudden vicious jab in the small of her back sent Paula plunging in front of it. Her arms flailed out, a woman screamed, the brakes screeched as the driver stood on them, and a hand caught one of Paula's arms, jerked her back so sharply that she fell on the curb.

The driver, white faced and shaking, got out of the cab. "What the hell are you trying to do?" he shouted.

"I was pushed," Paula said. "I was pushed."

The young woman who had saved her gave her a sharp look. "I guess you were at that, the way you fell forward."

"You want this cab or don't you?" the driver said and the man who had signaled him got in and drove off, eager to avoid being called as a witness.

The bus lumbered to a stop. To Paula's surprise, she and the woman who had pulled her away from the taxi were the only two people on the corner. The others were gone.

The woman grinned. "Afraid to be witnesses." she said grimly. "It always happens."

She helped Paula on the bus and sat beside her. Her name was Mary Andrews and she was a registered nurse. She gave Paula a card.

"Not," she admitted, "that I could help much. I'm sure you were pushed by the way you fell. If you'd been trying to pitch yourself under that taxi you'd have moved differently. But I didn't see him so I can't help you there. Who was it—the boy friend?"

"I don't know," Paula said. Her teeth were chattering as though she had a chill. "Someone was following me."

The nurse looked at her again. Obviously she did not believe her. She shrugged faintly. "Better get home and lie down. Wrap up warm. You've had a shock." She pressed the bell and stood up.

"Keep away from curbs," she said dryly.

At Forty-second Street Paula got off the bus, her legs still weak from shock, and walked toward Times Square. The sun was beating its way through the murk and the temperature was already beginning to soar.

Broadway, in the morning, is stripped of all its glamour. It is a sordid and ugly street of cheap shops, of theater ticket brokers, of orange juice bars, of movie theaters. On that sweltering June morning a barker stood outside a movie theater from which cold air poured enticingly onto the baking street, urging people to see the double-feature of horror films at half price until twelve o'clock.

Men went by, carrying their coats over their arms. A model with her hatbox, the badge of her trade, floated past, appearing to be unaware of the masculine eyes that followed her. The shops were empty, their clerks standing in the doorways. Even the legless pencil seller and the blind woman who sang nasally to the accordion had not yet appeared to take up their stations. Only *The New York Times* sign ran indefatigably around the tower, as though chasing its own tail, pouring out the misadventures of the world, punctuated by the correct time and the temperature. Eighty-seven degrees.

Paula bought a paper and turned by habit to the automat where she had eaten most of her meals for three months. She got coffee, watching fascinated to see whether just once it would overflow. It never did, of course. When the cup was filled, the stream of coffee stopped.

When she had drunk it at a small table she felt better. The trembling stopped, her heart steadied. She had built up the whole thing. Her nerves had been going to pieces for months and her talk with Miss Quarles had made them worse. The man in her room during the night, the

footsteps that had followed her, the shove that had so
nearly sent her under the taxi—there was no possible connection between them, just things one must expect in
overcrowded cities.

Anyhow, there was no reason on earth to think someone was deliberately trying—well, to hurt her. That's the
way people get queer, she told herself severely. She'd
never have had such an odd idea if Miss Quarles had not
said on the telephone, "I'd prefer to call it life insurance."
All along, that had made her uneasy.

Having disposed of her worries, Paula felt so much
better that she went back for more coffee and some toast.
Then she opened the paper.

Lenny Horgan had disappeared from the front page to
make room for the troubled state of the world; for "Pres-
ident declares . . ." "Mayor denies . . ." "Russia insists
. . ." "Woman killed in Central Park. The body of an
elderly woman, identified as Miss Helen Quarles, was
found shortly after midnight near the zoo in Central
Park. Her neck had been broken. The police believe mug-
gers . . ."

Paula put down the newspaper and pushed away the
toast. If there was one thing she was sure of it was that
Miss Quarles would never have ventured alone into Central Park at night. Never in the world. Someone had deliberately lured her there. Someone—the convict, Lenny
Horgan. "He hates me. I've been warned often enough.
I'm afraid."

Paula shook her head as though to clear it. Miss
Quarles had told her of her danger so that if she were
killed someone would know who had done it.

But why me, Paula thought. Why me?

She propped her head on her shaking hand. The key
in her lock—the jolt that had so nearly sent her pitching
in front of the taxi—

Call the police, she decided. Tell them—tell them
what? Tell them I am Paula Savage and I am mixed up
with a queer death. I know what they will say. "It isn't
the first time, is it?"

What then? Unexpectedly, she recalled hearing of a man who—what exactly had Graham said of him? "He isn't a detective. He's a fellow with the most insatiable curiosity I've ever seen. All you have to do is to let him scent a mystery and he'll follow it like a bloodhound."

Paula looked around for the telephone booths and opened the Manhattan directory. Her questing finger came to rest on the name "Potter, Hiram." The address was in Gramercy Park.

Four

As usual, there was an easel set up near the park fence and an artist was at work painting the four-story brick house with its white trim freshly painted and the iron grillwork that was like delicate lace around the shallow balcony outside long floor-to-ceiling windows. A summer tourist stopped to look over the painter's shoulder and then opened a camera that hung around his neck on a leather strap to take a picture of the house.

Gramercy Park is only a pocket handkerchief of a square set in the very heart of New York City. A high iron fence encloses its neat gravel paths, its carefully tended beds of flowers, its equally well-tended small children, supervised by nursemaids. The square is lined with hotels, apartment buildings that have big high-ceilinged rooms and wood-burning fireplaces, a couple of famous clubs and several private houses that in some dogged way have survived the pressure of the city to move on. A short block away in all directions New York roars in its accustomed manner, but here the sounds come muted.

In the library, which like most middle rooms in New York houses was without windows, Mr. Potter, a slight young man in his early thirties, with fair hair as smooth as glass and a mild pleasant face, sat in dusky coolness, carefully setting out on a chessboard the tiny figures he had unpacked from a big case. He examined each of the chessmen minutely and with delight. Months before, he had heard of this hand-carved Chinese set and, with his usual tenacity, he had stayed on its track ever since.

The dealer had groaned when Mr. Potter explained what he wanted. Only three sets were known to exist. One was in a museum, a second was part of a famous collection, the third had once been in the dealer's hands but he had sold it to a man who had moved out somewhere in the Middle West. The dealer didn't know his address and even if he did there was no reason to think the fellow would be willing to relinquish it, regardless of price.

The dealer had put both plump hands on his desk and looked at Mr. Potter, wishing, not for the first time, that he knew what went on behind that unrevealing face. Mr. Potter wore his inherited wealth like old clothes, comfortably and without ostentation. A nice guy to get along with, one who dropped in occasionally to look around, never made much of a fuss, and, before you knew it, he was as much at home in the place as if he lived or worked there. He never gave orders or threw his weight around and yet you knew, without knowing how you knew, that he packed a lot of authority and that, for all that misleading mildness, he carried considerable weight. A nice guy, the dealer thought again.

It was always hard for him to reconcile Mr. Potter's unobtrusive manner with the regularity with which he cropped up in the news. Not that the guy was a publicity seeker; he was one of those rare people who couldn't help making news.

"Now look here," the dealer said firmly, as though Mr. Potter had made some protest, though his customer simply watched him, his eyebrows arched in a question. "There are only three sets known to exist. That means both here and in free Europe. I don't say there isn't another somewhere in Red China but if you think—"

"I don't," Mr. Potter assured him mildly.

The dealer knew him too well to be assured. "This fellow who carved them never made more than four sets alike." He got up to unlock a case and took out a board on which some ivory chessmen had been placed. "Now there—" he began.

"Take away your red herring. It's the Chinese—"

"I know. I know. But I'm telling you. You'll never find a set."

"Oh, I wouldn't say that," Mr. Potter commented. "There's this fellow somewhere in the Middle West. How old is he?"

"Late sixties when I sold him the set. About ten years ago."

"There you are!"

"Where am I?" the other countered, on the defensive again.

"The chances are he has been gathered to his fathers and the estate has been broken up. So——"

"So?" the dealer echoed repressively, but already he knew that he had lost. By tomorrow he would be on the trail of that damned Chinese chess set. "Sometimes," he grumbled, "I wish you'd never got interested in collecting."

Mr. Potter shook his head. "You batten on me and then you complain."

"Batten! Just tracking down what you want keeps me thin."

"But not your bank account."

The dealer grinned. "The laborer," he said smugly, "is worthy of his hire."

He was, too. After a patient search, under the constant prodding of his customer, he had unearthed the set which Mr. Potter was unwrapping with such delight.

The chessmen were two inches high, all chess players, one bending over the board, absorbed; one smirking with pleasure; another signaling a move behind his back. Mr. Potter held a little slant-eyed mandarin with drooping mustaches and an air of timeless dignity, studying the details with enchantment. Then he sat it down in its proper square and drummed his fingers lightly on the table. Chess was endlessly fascinating but it was predictable. Well, that was what he wanted, wasn't it? No, damned if it was!

The trouble was that since a personal tragedy had shaken him out of the lethargy in which he had lived like a dead leaf on a stagnant pool, he had needed the stimulus of action as weaker men need alcohol. Crime had sought him out in the beginning, had forced him into violent activity, and had ripped apart the fabric of his staid life. After that, he was not sure whether he had been the sought or the seeking. Certainly, things happened to him. After becoming involved several times—too many times—in the excitement of the chase, he had realized that sooner or later he would get himself intangled in the kind of trouble there was no way out of. Each time he promised himself that he was through, that he would devote himself to collecting chessmen. But collecting wasn't enough. It was too passive. There was no challenge in it. It simply did not stir his imagination as an unsolved mystery did.

If Haydon had not broken his leg they would be in Maine now, preparing for a sailing trip down the coast. That was all that ailed him. His plans had been upset and he was at loose ends. It would—

The telephone rang and he picked it up. "Hiram Potter speaking."

"Oh, I'm so glad you are home. I was afraid—my name is Paula Savage. You won't know me but I know you through our mutual friend. Graham Collinge. Would you be very kind and let me come to see you? I won't take up much of your time."

It was a young voice and a lovely one, beautifully pitched. The operative words, he thought, judging by the strain she could not conceal, were "I was afraid."

"Come along if you like," he said and when he had put down the telephone he felt more cheerful.

Graham Collinge? Hardly a friend. A sensationally successful dramatist who always had a play on Broadway, a new one launched before an old one closed. They had met only a few times. The first time had been when Mr. Potter had tried to dig some information out of him when Nora Kendrick nearly got herself killed. Collinge had slipped out of his hands then but later they had got acquainted, though never close friends, nothing that would account for Collinge sending the girl with the strain in her voice to see him.

Mr. Potter wandered restlessly into the drawing room and looked across the street at the park. Already the trees were acquiring a dusty look. The artist had collected a small crowd and appeared to enjoy having an audience. He mixed his paints and squinted at the house with a self-conscious flourish.

A girl got out of a taxi and stood looking up at the house for a moment before she climbed the flight of steps to the white doorway with its delicate fanlight and rang the bell. She was a beauty, Mr. Potter decided enthusiastically.

He opened the door himself. "Miss Savage? I am Hiram Potter."

She stepped into the hallway with a magnificent crystal chandelier and a graceful white stairway that rose in soaring flight. There was a tesselated black-and-white marble floor, a long Venetian mirror above an ancient carved chest on which a slender silver vase held dark red roses whose fragrance filled the air.

Mr. Potter stood back to let her precede him through the drawing room into the library, where a fan stirred the air almost soundlessly.

"It's cooler in here. I believe you'll find that chair comfortable."

"You are very kind to see me," Paula began when he had seated himself behind the small table on which the chessmen had been placed. "There's no excuse for me at all except—Graham Collinge talked a lot about you one evening. He told me how you got Nora Kendrick out of that terrible mess last year. So, though I realize you were an old friend of hers and you had a reason for helping her—"

When he saw that she had come to a full stop, Mr. Potter gave her a swift look. She was not really beautiful but she gave an illusion of beauty, a tall girl with those little hollows under the cheekbones that photograph so well. Her bronze hair seemed to spring up from her forehead. Her eyes were a deep brown and nicely set but there were dark shadows under them. Illness? Dissipation?

Lack of sleep? The girl looked as though she had not slept for a week. Her long hands, ringless but with a faint indentation on the ring finger of the left hand, gripped the arms of her chair. Her yellow linen dress was simple and becoming but it hadn't cost more than twenty dollars.

She became aware of his scrutiny and her hands relaxed, one dropped lightly into her lap, the other turned in an unexpectedly eloquent gesture toward him. Actress, he decided.

"I take it," he said, "that you are in a terrible mess."

"And you wonder, quite justifiably, what business it is of yours."

He didn't like the white line around her mouth or the sudden nervous jerk that twitched the corners of her lips.

"Actually," he admitted, "I've been wondering what in heaven's name I was going to do with myself today. I'm at loose ends. Let's have some coffee, shall we? Hot coffee," he added, remembering how cold her fingers had been when they shook hands. Shock, perhaps.

He rang the bell and when a stout Italian wearing a crisp white jacket came to the door he said, "Tito, bring us some coffee, will you? And muffins."

"You see," Paula began, her hands quiet now that she was about to speak.

"Let's wait for the coffee, shall we? Unless you are in a hurry to go somewhere else."

"Why no," Paula said with a kind of astonishment. "I have nowhere else to go at all."

"Are you interested in chess?" Mr. Potter showed her the pieces, one by one, keeping the conversation firmly on the stately little mandarins and his long search for them while Paula drank coffee and ate two muffins. Then, when he had lighted her cigarette, he asked, "Better?"

She had a delightful smile. "Much better. I didn't eat any breakfast. When I saw that story in the morning paper and realized she had been murdered and someone was trying to kill me, I was frightened almost out of my wits."

"All right," Mr. Potter admitted after a pause, "you have astonished me." He picked up a tiny chessman and turned it around in his fingers. "Why did you come to me, Miss Savage, instead of going to the police?"

She smiled ruefully and, before she spoke, he knew she was going to lie to him. "Because I haven't a scrap of evidence. They would be polite and make notes and ease me out of there. I thought you had imagination."

"That," Mr. Potter assured her feelingly, "is my curse. Look here, Miss Savage, we mustn't have any misunderstandings." He spoke carefully in order to make his warning clear. "I don't want you to tell me anything that you might regret later. If you are involved—that is, if there is anything the police should know, I couldn't just keep silent, you know."

She surprised him by saying, "That suits me fine. Right now, I am scared half out of my mind and I don't know what on earth to do."

"Then suppose you tell me about it."

She told him about the advertisement and her interview with Miss Quarles, pausing to recollect the older woman's exact words, remembering uneasily the impression they had made on her, fearing that she was having the same effect on Mr. Potter, telling of Miss Quarles's terror of Lenny Horgan and ending with the telephone conversation she had overheard.

Mr. Potter watched her in fascination. Through the inflection of her voice, the nervous fluttering gestures, the changing expression of her face, the rigidity of her pose, she evoked vividly the taut gushing old woman. It was an incredible performance.

When he spoke, however, he made no comment on her evocation of Helen Quarles. He was not sure how much of it had been deliberate, how much an unconscious imitation.

"Life insurance," he echoed slowly. "How did she strike you, Miss Savage?"

Paula looked at him, uncertain of his meaning.

"Was she level-headed or hysterical? The kind who imagines things or the kind who reports them literally? Under other circumstances would you be inclined to rely on anything she told you?"

"No," Paula admitted frankly, "I wouldn't. The woman was neurotic. But I don't think—I didn't think even then —that her fear was imaginary."

"Why not?"

Paula's hand made a groping gesture, as though seeking for an answer. "Because she was—she felt guilty, for some reason, about the testimony she had given. I can't explain why that made her fear seem more credible, more believable. But it did. Anyhow," she added flatly, "I have to believe her now. Because the woman is dead and someone killed her."

Mr. Potter reached for the morning paper and she pointed out the item for him. When he had finished it, he looked up. "There's no reference to the fact that she was the key witness in the Horgan murder trial or even that she had any association with it."

"Just the same—"

"Do you have any idea, Miss Savage, how many people claim to be involved in murders they know nothing about, year after year? Either through some curious sort of exhibitionism or some distorted sense of guilt, a kind of need to be punished."

"But she is dead," Paula said stubbornly.

"Mugged." When Paula shook her head he asked, "Why couldn't it have happened that way?"

"Because she was an exceptionally timid woman. New York terrified her. She would never have gone to Central Park alone at night. Never."

"All right," he said. "Go on. We'll assume for a moment that Miss Quarles was right, that Lenny Horgan murdered her the night he was released from prison in a spirit of revenge that he had nursed for twenty years. Twenty years, Miss Savage! So deep a hatred that he was prepared to return to prison, to go to the death house, to satisfy it. I find that more than I can swallow. And on top of that we have to explain why a woman who was

paralyzed with terror at the very thought of encounter-
ing Horgan agreed to meet him, alone and at night, in
Central Park."

Paula stood up. "I'm sorry to have imposed on you, to
have taken up so much of your," she glanced at the
chessmen, "valuable time," she finished bitterly.

He was on his feet, too. "Please, Miss Savage. Don't
go yet. Let's talk it over."

There were spots of angry color burning in her cheeks.
"But you don't believe a word I say. You don't—"

"I don't know what to believe," he admitted, "but I
have an open mind." Gently he pushed her back into her
chair. "Red-headed women alarm me," he complained.
"They fly off the handle."

"I'm not red—" She smiled reluctantly. "Sorry. I am
and I do. And it was a perfectly reasonable question. Actually it seems to me the last thing on earth Miss Quarles
would have done."

"It was the last thing she did," he reminded her. "Well,
we'll let Miss Quarles's inexplicable behavior go for a moment and get back to you. Are you really afraid that
someone will try to kill you because of that telephone
conversation you overheard?"

"No," she said deliberately, and she was cold again,
"I'm afraid because someone—only why do we say someone when we mean Lenny Horgan?—has already tried to
kill me."

"That's a good curtain line," he commented and saw
that he had startled her. "I'm all agog. Tell me."

Paula had been dramatic in her account of the disturb-
ing interview with Miss Quarles but Mr. Potter's remark
about the curtain line had thrown her off balance. She
made a conscious effort not to dramatize, to keep her account as simple and factual as she could. She was aware,
with a feeling of irony, that she was less convincing when
she held herself to unadorned fact.

As she looked at Mr. Potter she felt a kind of blank
discouragement. Graham Collinge had spoken of him as
though he were extraordinary and he was just—mild.

Mr. Potter picked up a tiny chess player and stared at it as though seeking counsel for the next move. The girl was overwrought. He did not think she had lied to him, except about the police, though she was holding back a lot, choosing her words carefully. Cautious. Very cautious. Something was bothering her like hell. Something had been bothering her for a long time. Shadows like those under her very pretty eyes didn't come overnight.

But what did it amount to? She had talked to the neurotic Quarles woman who had babbled not of green fields but of murder and had died violently. Coincidence? Possibly. Possibly not. Though the idea that a frightened woman had gone into the park at night to meet the man who frightened her was difficult to credit.

The girl had been awakened by a thunder storm and found her door unlocked. She thought someone had followed her down the street. She thought someone had pushed her in front of a taxi. He could imagine the police listening to that story.

"Just what," he asked, "did you think I could do for you, Miss Savage?"

She looked at him for a moment in silence. He had very intelligent eyes. For the first time she believed that, some way or other, he might be able to help her. Because he was so unlike the reckless adventurer she had conjured up from Graham Collinge's glowing account, she had discounted his abilities. Mr. Potter would take risks, she could believe that, but they would never be pointless, never an adolescent's thrill-seeking; which accounted for most adventurers, whatever their age. His risks would be calculated. And he would bring a freshness of viewpoint to anything he attempted. He was skeptical, perhaps, but genuinely interested and there was a refreshing absence of conceit in him. He wouldn't, she thought, hesitate to try new ideas, which was a rare quality. He wouldn't even mind being proved wrong, which was much rarer.

"I don't really know," she admitted. "I told you there is no evidence, nothing to go on. Except the fact that Miss Quarles is dead. And I don't want to die, Mr. Pot-

ter. Not that way. Not furtively in the dark. And I don't
want to live wondering when it is going to happen. Keeping away from curbs, as the nurse told me."

"Of course," Mr. Potter said, "the chances are ten to
one that Miss Quarles's murder—if it was a murder—had
no connection whatever with the fact that someone acci-
dentally or deliberately pushed you in front of a taxi this
morning. But we'll look at the one-to-ten chance. We'll
assume, just to make it interesting, that Miss Quarles told
her murderer about you, that he got your address from
her purse, that he got a fistful of keys and came along
to take a look at you, so that he could identify you later,
that he followed you in the morning, looking for a chance
to eliminate you and, being an opportunist, seized his
chance to push you under a taxi. It's pretty far-fetched,
it's about impossible to prove, but let's assume that it is
true."

"A game," Paula said. "It's a game to you. I've become
involved by sheer accident in this ugly business—"

Mr. Potter grinned and she found something warm and
likable in the young man who, at first, appeared so cool
and detached.

"There," he told her cheerfully, "we are fellow suf-
ferers, you and I. Except that you are new to it." But are
you, he wondered. "And I am an old hand. If I were to
tell you some of the things I've been involved in—well,
let's go over it again, from the very beginning."

An hour later, Paula leaned back in her chair, exhausted. "If the third degree is anything like this—"

"I like to get the facts straight," Mr. Potter said apologetically.

"Straight!"

He laughed at her outraged expression. "At least, I
won't ask you to go through all that again. And I had to
be sure you remembered and told me everything."

"By this time I've told you everything I ever knew in
my life."

"Oh, no," Mr. Potter said calmly, "you've held back
quite a lot. 'What seest thou else in the dark backward

and abysm of Time?' " He held up his hand as she began to speak. "Don't blow up now. We'll have a gin and tonic or maybe two and then some lunch."

"Oh, I can't—"

"Of course you can. Anyhow, we have to make some plans."

"What sort of plans?" she asked doubtfully.

He looked at her in some surprise. "For going to Coxbury, of course."

"But I'm not—"

"Oh, yes you are."

"If you think for one moment," Paula sputtered, "that I am going to stick my head into the lion's mouth, be dangled like a piece of live bait—"

"You sound like a teakettle boiling over. Cool off. Nothing is going to happen. I'll be there to keep an eye on you." He handed her a tall frosty glass that tinkled cheerfully of ice. "Drink up."

"Why do you want me to go to Coxbury? What could possibly be gained by it?"

"Because you've convinced me," he said. "I believe Miss Quarles was deliberately lured to Central Park and murdered. You've convinced me that someone tried to get rid of you this morning. I find it hard to believe two people would have a motive for—ah—eliminating you. And since Miss Quarles had no acquaintances in this country except in Coxbury, we are going there."

While she ate lunch in the dining room at the back of the house that looked out on a small garden, Paula asked, "Have you any ideas?"

"One, but it is nebulous and pretty far fetched."

"Do you think I am in danger?"

Mr. Potter answered her obliquely. "There's one thing about danger. The only way to cope is to face the damned thing. Now I'll tell you what we're going to try to do."

Five

"Go away," the detective said.

Mr. Potter grinned at him, pulled a chair across the desk and offered his cigarette case.

The detective accepted a light. "I knew it," he said gloomily. "I should have taken my vacation in June instead of waiting for August. I'd have missed the heat wave and I'd have missed you."

"I've got something for you," Mr. Potter said cheerfully.

"I'll bet you have. A headache. Every time you come ambling in here you stir up trouble. I've never figured out what it is about you, Potter. Someone was talking about you the other day. Said you were a catalytic agent; take two harmless ingredients, stir in a dash of Potter, and you get trouble. Damn it, whenever you get involved in a case, something happens." He was half amused, half serious. "Well, what have you got this time?"

"Murder," Mr. Potter told him. "Attempted murder."

"Which?"

"Both." He pushed across the table the news item from the morning paper and tapped it with his finger.

O'Toole read it. "Ordinary mugging. Are you trying to make something of it?"

Mr. Potter nodded. "She was in her sixties and afraid of New York. She would never have ventured into Central Park alone at night."

"You knew her?"

"Knew of her."

"But she did—Oh, I take it the operative word is 'alone.'" The detective re-read the clipping. "Is that just your idea or are you sure of your facts?"

"Reasonably sure."

The detective gave him a keen look and nodded. "That's good enough for me. But damn it all, the case is nicely accounted for and then you come along—" He lifted the telephone and talked for a few moments.

"She wasn't robbed," he told Mr. Potter slowly. "Her handbag was beside her. Money, identification, all the usual junk a woman carries."

"Was there," Mr. Potter asked, "a slip of paper in a zippered compartment with a woman's name, address and telephone number?"

O'Toole studied him again and then made another call. No such memorandum had been found. The zippered compartment was empty.

"Now then," he said, "suppose you tell me why you came charging in here on a hot day to bring the glad tidings that this Miss Quarles had been murdered."

"Helen Quarles," Mr. Potter told him, "was the key witness in the Horgan murder trial. She was the only witness. She had been warned for years that if Horgan was ever released he intended to kill her."

"And he got out yesterday." The detective sat rubbing his forehead. "That wasn't our case. Connecticut. And before I was even on the force. The kid was a chess prodigy. That's chiefly why I remember it. I had an uncle who was trying to teach me the game and telling me about this Lenny Horgan. Then the kid murdered a girl and I had the laugh on my uncle. That ended the chess sessions."

"Just what did happen?"

"Horgan strangled this chick in a movie theater somewhere in Connecticut back in the summer of 1938." He added in a half-hearted hope that this would discourage Mr. Potter, "There was no mystery about it at all. No question that he did it. There was only one odd thing; no one could figure out why he killed her. He never would say why."

"Not a sex crime?"

The detective raised astonished eyebrows. "In a crowded movie theater? The girl was no virgin, that's for sure. But she wasn't pregnant. No one ever knew why the kid did it. A psychiatrist brought in by his lawyer tried to make a lot of that but the kid was sane enough. He just wasn't talking."

The detective looked down at the news item again. "The cop who found the Quarles woman thought it was one of those muggings we get every so often. Hell, we haven't enough cops to patrol every dark path in every city park. Why don't women have sense enough to stay out of them?"

"That's the biggest question, so far as I can see," Mr. Potter admitted. "She was timid and yet she went to Central Park at night."

"What put you onto this?"

Mr. Potter told him in detail.

The detective listened thoughtfully. "The old woman tells this girl that Horgan wants to kill her and then gets her neck broken in Central Park. It could be coincidence. It could still be a routine mugging—and the guy lost his nerve when he saw he had killed her and ran without taking her handbag, probably afraid to touch it."

"If he was afraid to touch it, what happened to the slip of paper with Paula Savage's name and address on it?"

The detective shrugged. "We'll check on Horgan and see where he was last night. But a twenty-year grudge! Hell, the boy wasn't a psychopath. And how can we prove anything, even if he hasn't an air-tight alibi as he's almost sure to have on his first night out of prison. He was probably surrounded by rejoicing family and friends."

"When was the woman killed?"

"Some time between nine and ten. Before the storm. Her clothes were soaked except where she'd fallen. That part was dry and so was the ground under her."

"Then her murderer found the address in the zipper pocket, where everyone knew she kept memoranda, and

got to Paula Savage's apartment house during the storm.
The timing is all right."

"Who is this Savage woman who fed you the soap op-
era?"

Mr. Potter didn't know. He had never seen her before.
She had reached his house in a state of shock, badly
shaken by her narrow escape.

"Yeah, it's all nice and vague, isn't it?"

"Isn't that," Mr. Potter suggested, "the way a clever
man would plan it? So that it would look accidental?"

"Maybe. Though they always make mistakes."

"You are talking," Mr. Potter reminded him, "about
the ones you catch."

"Yeah. But this is like trying to get hold of a fistful of
fog. Do you know how I see it, Potter? A good-looking
girl who knew your weakness for mysteries dangled a
nice hunk of bait in front of you and you swallowed it
hook, line and sinker."

"But why would she do that?"

The detective was amused. "In some ways, you are kind
of dumb. It never struck you, I suppose, that you are one
hell of a wealthy guy, a bachelor, and you haven't a hare
lip or a club foot."

Mr. Potter looked at him helplessly. Then he laughed.
"I don't know much about Paula Savage and I wouldn't
be surprised if there is quite a lot to learn. But whatever
her object in coming to see me may have been, it was
not matrimony."

"You can tell, I suppose," the detective said dryly. "All
women are an open book to you."

Belatedly, he realized that he had blundered, but
though Mr. Potter's face stiffened he answered quietly
enough, "I know a state of shock when I see one."

O'Toole, who had known Mr. Potter a long time and
had a feeling which was akin to hero worship for him,
was still angry with himself. What a fool he was to have
forgotten the girl Mr. Potter had been in love with, the
girl who was shut up for life somewhere as a homicidal

maniac. Mr. Potter never referred to her but, though he was highly eligible, he had not married. It must have cut very deep.

"We'll look up this Paula Savage. She might have a record."

"She won't have," Mr. Potter said confidently. Then he looked at his friend in a wild surmise. "She may at that. Anyhow, I have one way of checking on her."

"How's that?"

"Graham Collinge. She knows him. That is why she came to me."

But was it, Mr. Potter wondered. There had been something in her manner—she had shied away from the police. Well, it wasn't his job to hound frightened women. Let them check on her for themselves.

He grinned. "She thought I had imagination."

The detective snorted. "Imagination! That's one way of putting it. Who is this Collinge? Is he the one who writes plays where everything is a symbol for something else and they all go to hell in the end? Highbrow stuff?" The telephone rang and he became involved. It looked like a long involvement.

Mr. Potter got up. "I'll keep in touch and I'll see you have my Connecticut address."

"Hey, give me the Savage woman's address."

"She'll be in Coxbury, too. Care of Mr. Ed Morison."

"Hell, Potter, you can't do that—drag the girl into this thing."

"She's already in it," Mr. Potter reminded him. "And if she isn't on the spot I don't see how we can smoke out our man. We've got to make something happen."

The detective groaned. "Here we go again! You might look up your Trooper friend in Connecticut. The Horgan murder was their case. We'll get cracking on it here but it's the kind of case I hate. Nothing to go on but guess-work. No evidence. No way I can see of proving the woman wasn't mugged. I'd hate to think what a defense attorney would do to it."

Mr. Potter waved and went out. The street was blister-

ingly hot and he moved over to the shady side, entered a
cigar store and found a telephone booth.

II

Graham Collinge sounded irritable when he answered
the telephone and worried after Mr. Potter told him who
he was. There was a marked pause before he suggested,
with a total lack of enthusiasm, that Mr. Potter drop in
to see him.

The building in which the playwright had a penthouse
was on Central Park South. A Japanese houseman admitted Mr. Potter. Graham Collinge, in silk pajamas and a
pongee robe, was lying on a low couch in an air-cooled
room that looked down in Central Park. A kingsize ash-
tray filled with cigarette butts was on the floor within
easy reach of his hand and he held a blue-bound play-
script.

He got up to shake hands and offered his guest a drink,
which the latter refused. For a few minutes the two men
sparred amiably. Yes, it was a new play, just back from
the typing bureau. A departure for him, an adaptation
from a novel. It had been an interesting experiment but
he'd never do it again. The values, the emphases were too
different. The novelist had a hundred thousand words in
which to build a character and the playwright less than
thirty thousand. You couldn't get across all the shades
of meaning.

But he had live people, Mr. Potter reminded him. The
inflection of a voice, the motion of a hand, a fleeting expression were worth whole chapters. They revealed things
in a flash. He recalled Paula Savage's brilliant evocation
of a neurotic old woman.

"When you can - get the right cast, yes," Collinge
agreed. "But the people you want are usually in another
play or under contract in Hollywood or serving a sentence on TV. Or they got typed somewhere along the
line and no one thinks of them in any other kind of rôle."

He broke off to say, "But you didn't rout me out on a

stinker of a day like this to talk shop. Not my kind of shop, anyhow."

"No," Mr. Potter admitted, "I came to talk to you about Paula Savage."

Collinge blinked his surprise. "Well, I'll be damned! I've been searching my conscience ever since you called, wondering what was up and going over my friends and acquaintances, one by one, trying to figure out—but I never thought of Paula Savage."

"Never thought of her in difficulties, you mean?" With a glance at his host's revealing face, Mr. Potter said, "Well, well. A hit. A palpable hit. How well do you know her?"

Collinge grinned. "Over to you, brother. I'm not talking until I know what this is all about. And I mean all." His manner was friendly but he meant what he said.

Remembering a time when the playwright had disappeared from a restaurant and gone to earth rather than betray a friend's confidence, Mr. Potter surrendered.

"That's fair enough. I'm not giving away any secrets. She assumed that I would use what she told me, sooner or later." For a second time in a couple of hours Mr. Potter repeated Paula Savage's story. "Well, there it is," he concluded.

Collinge nodded noncommittally. "It sounds as though the poor girl has got herself in the devil of a mess. You know, it seems to me that some people—" He broke off. "Why didn't she tell me she needed a job that bad? I could have used her in my last play. Actually, I could use her in this one," and he tapped the typescript. "If only—" He checked himself again. "Where is she now, do you know?"

Mr. Potter consulted his watch. "Somewhere around Hawthorne Circle, I suppose, on her way to Coxbury."

"No!" Collinge leaped to his feet and something about his expression brought Mr. Potter up, alert and watchful. "Damn it, just because you get a kick out of these things you've sent that poor girl—"

"Oh, stop towering over me," Mr. Potter complained.

"Did you think what might happen—"

"I'll be there myself. And I'll alert the State Troopers. She will be amply protected."

Collinge felt rather silly, glowering down at Mr. Potter's calm face and he subsided into a chair. "What's the idea?" he asked more quietly.

"I'm going to try to smoke out a murderer—if there was a murder, if I'm not chasing a will o' the wisp. That's why I came to see you."

"But I don't know the first thing about Lenny Horgan. Oh, the name is familiar and I saw the story yesterday that he was released from prison but—" Collinge's jaw dropped. "Sweet Jesus! Did you think, because my apartment is on the park—"

Mr. Potter began to laugh and after a while Collinge joined in, relieved but puzzled.

"Then why—?"

"Because you know Paula Savage and I don't. How reliable is she? That story of hers—how much is plain fact, how much is theater? Before I go off the deep end I'd like to know how much water there is in the pool." Mr. Potter listened to himself in considerable surprise. "I sound just like Madison Avenue."

"The damned thing is insidious," Collinge said gloomily. "I have to watch it all the time." He began to walk up and down the room, hands in the pockets of his robe, eyes on the modern rug with its geometrical design in bold colors. Now and then, he paused to look sharply at his quiet but observant guest; then he continued his pacing while he worked out some problem in his mind.

Mr. Potter waited with unruffled patience. Collinge was a completely honorable man and he was also an exceptionally loyal one. Apparently, the two factors were engaged in battle. In the long run, though he might attempt to withhold information, Mr. Potter was positive that he would not lie.

At length the playwright stopped in front of Mr. Potter. "I'd say there is plenty of water. Paula is singularly truthful, painfully truthful. She doesn't need to dramatize things."

"She's an actress."

"Yes," Collinge said impatiently, "of course she's an actress, but she keeps it for the stage. The good ones do. With her looks and charm and attraction for men she never needed to—build things. Anyhow, it isn't in her nature. She is straightforward and modest and honest. Too damned honest, if you ask me."

"I am asking you," Mr. Potter reminded him.

Collinge grinned reluctantly. "All right. But there's not much I can tell you. Paula is a girl from the Middle West who went into dramatics in college, got a job in summer stock and found that acting was what she wanted. She didn't go back to school. Instead, she joined an excellent Shakespeare repertory theater for the experience—"

"That accounts for her beautiful enunciation," Mr. Potter interrupted. "I'm willing to bet she's one of the few who can read the lines without chanting them and communicate all their beauty in natural-sounding speech."

"She is," Collinge agreed. "Well, she married. That's what goofed things up. She married Derek Savage, a guy who was assistant director in the theater. Good looking in a soft sort of way, all profile and ego. He was a frustrated actor if I ever saw one but he just didn't have it. All he was good for was to—"

"Swell a progress," Mr. Potter suggested.

Collinge nodded moodily. "He poulticed his bruised little ego by making love to the admiring ladies who hang around stage doors, particularly in art colonies, but he was wildly jealous of Paula who is the kind to stick to a bad bargain. I don't know what makes women do it. Pride? Duty? Pity? Anyhow, she led a rotten life with him."

He broke off to say, "By the way, I picked up these side lights from other people. Paula never said a word. Anyhow, when Derek Savage—died, she just folded up her tent and disappeared. I ran into her in a theater lobby not long ago and dragged her off for a drink. She told me nothing about herself."

He added, with a challenge in his voice, "That's all I know."

Mr. Potter shook his head. "Give!" he said.

Collinge kicked at the rug with his slippered foot. Then he opened a cupboard below his bookshelves and pawed through a stack of old theatrical magazines. He pulled one out and handed it to Mr. Potter, open at an article headed, "Her Most Dramatic Rôle." There was a news picture of a courtroom and under it the words: "Paula Savage (in dark glasses) at inquest into her husband's death."

Mr. Potter read the story in growing wonder at the language. "The glamorous actress . . . From thrilling romance to grim tragedy . . . Fascinating Derek, her boy-husband . . . Paula, white and tearless, tells of the events that lead to the fatal accident . . . Hysterical woman screams, 'You murderess!' "

"How much of this," he asked at length, "is true?"

Collinge sighed. "About half, I should say. If Paula hadn't been such an awful fool—"

"But which half?" Mr. Potter insisted.

III

There was a chill in the air when the shabby Volkswagen parked neatly beside a State Police car at the red barn. Mr. Potter might easily have passed the barn itself without a second glance, as none of Molly's landmarks were visible to the naked eye. What caught his attention was the unexpected sight of two oil paintings propped up in a vegetable stand, marked, "For Sale—inquire within."

Mr. Potter laughed and peered out of the Volkswagen at the barn. There was a big sign in front: "Antiques—Good and Bad." Above were casement windows wide open to the breeze and voices floated out of the windows.

Floated? One of them blasted with the roar of a maddened bull. The Jepsons were at it again, he decided with pleasure.

". . . a smock? Get it straight. Never will I be caught dead painting in a smock."

"I just thought," the second voice began, and Mr. Potter grinned to himself. When Molly got that helpless tone, Kurt was sunk. "I was thinking about cleaning bills. A smock would be so nice for saving your clothes—so practical."

"And how often do we send blue jeans to the cleaner? I wash them myself. I know you and your tortuous mind. The first step, that's what it is. The entering wedge. First a smock, then a beret, and then—" A yelp.

"Kurt! What's the matter?" his wife asked anxiously.

"I just realized," he said, his tone menacing. "The casual way you said this morning, 'Oh, don't bother to shave.' You know what, Captain? She's aiming to have me grow a beard! That's what. Creeping up on it, little by little. Undermining my defenses."

Mr. Potter was laughing as he climbed the outside stairs to the second floor of the converted barn. The door stood open. There were three people sitting around a small table covered by a checkered red-and-white cloth, with spaghetti, tossed salad, crusty bread, and a straw-covered bottle of red wine before them.

"It's all right, Captain Foote," he called reassuringly. "It blows off in steam. No one ever gets hurt."

A small brown girl in a playsuit hurled herself exuberantly into his arms. "Hiram! How swell. You're just in time for supper."

"A disgusting exhibition," the tall slim man in a red shirt and blue jeans remarked bitterly. "Let him go, Molly. You're half strangling the guy. Fight her off," he advised. "That's what I do."

Mr. Potter emerged laughing from Molly's embrace, shook hands with Kurt Jepson and turned to greet the tall, military looking man with the bronzed face, who had been watching in amusement.

"I should have warned you about eating here," he said, looking with open suspicion at the table. "Molly has the most harrowing ideas about nutrition."

"At least this is honest food," Kurt said. "Poor but honest. I put my foot down. 'Molly,' I said in ringing tones, 'we will live in that barn, leaky roof and squirrels and all; we will waylay and rob the innocent passer-by, luring him to his destruction with the siren call of antiques; we will roll our own cigarettes. But I will not, repeat will not, make an exclusive diet of soy beans.'"

"The article proved they have everything you need for nutrition. And they're so cheap," Molly mourned. "Hiram, I'm afraid the spaghetti is a little cold."

"I had dinner an hour ago."

"Is that why you are late?"

"I am late because I followed your directions. For instance, turn right at a white church. What white church?"

"Why—oh, I forgot. You can't see it from the road, can you?"

"You cannot," Mr. Potter told her grimly.

Until Captain Foote of the Connecticut State Police had finished eating, the Jepsons kept up a barrage of banter. There was nothing in their manner to suggest that they were surprised by the presence of a police officer at their table. At length, Mr. Potter, seeing Foote's surreptitious look at his watch, said, "I liked your art gallery out there."

"Out where?" Jepson turned to look at his wife. "Molly, did you—"

"Well," she said defiantly, "how can people buy them if they don't see them?"

"You come with me!" He grabbed her wrist and dragged her from the room. Kurt Jepson was not slow at taking a hint. The two men could hear them bickering and laughing as they went out to the vegetable stand beside the highway.

"That's a nice young couple," the captain said. "You don't often see them as happy as that. When I got here and said I was to meet you they took me in as though we were old friends, and first thing I knew I was winding spaghetti on my fork. Are they really so poor?"

Mr. Potter laughed. "Kurt's father is Hans Jepson, the tool manufacturer. He wanted Kurt in the business and Kurt wanted to paint. Finally, the old man gave him ten thousand dollars with the understanding that when it is spent he has to go into the business unless he has proved that he can paint pictures that people will buy. Molly thinks up the most horrifying and catastrophic ways of stretching money."

"How much would he have if he gave this up?"

"Maybe sixty thousand a year until the old man dies."

"And Mrs. Jepson doesn't want it?" Foote was incredulous.

"She likes the guy," Mr. Potter said lightly, "and he likes to paint, so—"

The captain smiled. "A nice young couple," he repeated. The smile faded. "Now what's all this about Lenny Horgan?"

For the third and, he hoped, the last time, Mr. Potter told his story. Captain Foote listened intently.

"I remember Helen Quarles," he said at length. "I knew all the people in the Horgan case because I've lived around here my whole life. Quarles was one of those twittery women. No harm in her but always complaining about dangerous dogs and 'Officer, I saw a snake' and we ought to patrol Coxbury every hour all night. I was in court when she testified and she looked like death. She was a great friend of young Horgan's mother and she hated doing it."

He lighted a cigarette. "So she got herself killed in Central Park last night. You know, Mr. Potter, what beats me is how anyone persuaded her to go there. Why, even in Coxbury she didn't like to go out alone, though it has always been safe as churches, and she was a lot younger then."

"That's the puzzle," Mr. Potter agreed. "Incidentally, do you know why she couldn't rent her cottage?"

Captain Foote rubbed his jaw. "She rented it for years.

But then—say, that's an odd thing. I don't know why it never struck me before. There is practically no pilfering or housebreaking around here. Mostly traffic problems like everywhere else. But the Quarles cottage has been broken into every summer and ransacked. So far as I know, nothing was ever taken, but people didn't like it. Word got around, and the last few years no one would rent the place. What has that to do—?"

Mr. Potter didn't know. He had got to wondering why she had been unable to rent the house. Just a queer fact, that was all.

"What strikes me as queer," Captain Foote admitted, "is Lenny having it in for Miss Quarles. It's all out of character." He jabbed at his cigarette. "In a way, all this is out of character. Of course, there's not a shred of proof Lenny killed Miss Quarles or tried to kill this Miss Savage."

"I know," Mr. Potter agreed. "The New York police pointed that out to me. They think I've got hold of a mare's nest."

"Anyhow, it's not in our jurisdiction. It's New York's problem. Unless they ask—" Foote saw Mr. Potter's expression. "Oh, we'll keep an eye on your Miss Savage. But if she is going to stay at the Morison house she ought to be safe enough."

"A good man, is he?"

"Morison? Why Ed Morison is Coxbury. Morisons and Coxes—his mother was a Cox—always have been Coxbury. They don't come better. The new lot, the summer people, aren't the same breed. Just the privileges without the responsibilities. That sort. Miss Savage will be all right at Morison's. I don't mean he can protect her physically—he is almost incapacitated by arthritis—but people aren't going to harm anyone under his roof. Anyhow, his nephew is back, that Bentwick fellow. I saw him drive past at noon in one of those fancy foreign sports jobs. So there will be a vigorous man in the house."

Captain Foote laughed without humor. "As soon as word gets out that the old man is ailing, Bentwick comes steaming up to find out what's going. But I think the old man is shrewd enough to see through that."

He sighed. "Of course, you understand there is nothing we can do here except keep our eyes open." He added slowly, "I checked up after you called. Horgan's mother got permission to take him to New York last night to get away from reporters." He nodded as he saw Mr. Potter's expression. "Yup. He was there. But it's funny. I'd never figure Horgan for a thing like that."

"He killed once before," Mr. Potter reminded him.

"Yes, I know. But he wasn't tough. He was all broken up. He wasn't criminal caliber. It was a one-shot, as most murders are. At least, I'd have said so. And when I knew he was getting out, I'd never have said Lenny would be the one—I mean—"

"I wish to God," he burst out, "Lenny Horgan wasn't coming back to Coxbury. This is a kindly sort of place on the whole—oh, a lot of backbiting and making the most of gossip, all that, but usually they rally round when people are in trouble. But there is something I can't put my finger on. I don't like the attitude of the villagers. I can smell trouble coming. I wouldn't like to be in Lenny Horgan's shoes, and that's a fact."

Six

The road was narrow and tree-lined. Like most Connecticut roads it went up and down hill, curving always. At every turn there was a new vista: the distant view of misty blue hills, a white church spire glimpsed through green foliage, a neat farm on rolling land with a bright red barn and a stone fence.

Then, after sounding her horn, Paula rounded the blind curve cautiously and stopped the car in sheer surprise. Behind her the land was green and fertile. Here it was barren, torn in great channels. A harmless looking stream that sparkled in sunlight wandered over a bed of pebbles where rushing waters had carved canyons through the land. The topsoil was gone. Nothing remained but the rocks that lie so close to the surface in Connecticut, and here and there the jagged roots of a great fallen tree that pointed to the sky.

Paula drove on more slowly. A neat plaque announced: "Entering Coxbury. Drive slow." The road branched here. The blacktop curved up to the right, the dirt road went down to the left, plunging steeply downhill to what remained of the old village: a few dozen houses, a white church, a stone chimney that stood alone near the river, a town hall with an unexpectedly impressive clock tower.

Paula hesitated at the point of the V and then, remembering Mr. Potter's instructions, took the road up the hill to the new village. "Pick up local gossip first, if you can. Try the general store," he had told her, "or the post office."

She was gambling a lot on Mr. Potter. An awful lot. She was not clear just how he had maneuvered her into agreeing to come to Coxbury, to smoke out a man who had killed two women and tried to kill her. It was a crazy thing to do and yet Mr. Potter was very sane. He had better be, she thought grimly.

There were more customers in the general store than she had expected: a sprinkling of farmers, standing in leisurely talk beside a display of garden tools, half a dozen women in house dresses with brown paper bags of groceries in their arms, looking at the flats of pansies and petunias and asters that made an obstacle race of the open porch. Something about them struck Paula as odd. Then she realized that they all seemed to be waiting.

As she picked her way around the flats there was a general cessation of talk while they looked her over, frankly and slowly. When she was inside, the talk broke out again, clearly audible through the open door.

"So I told her right then and there, 'Look here, young lady, you aren't going to the movies at night this summer, not unless you are with a whole crowd.' Well, she's home sulking and my husband thinks I am silly but—"

"I know how you feel. I had my husband buy some real good locks in Hartford as soon as I heard the news."

"Locks?" said the first woman. "I don't know as I'd do that. It's not as though Lenny Horgan was ever a thief. It was just—girls."

"You never can tell," the second replied darkly. "I won't draw an easy breath as long as he's in Coxbury, and I'm not the only one either."

"One thing sure. He'd never have got out of prison if his stepfather had lived. Forrest Bulow blocked every attempt to free him. I used to think Forrest was a terribly hard man, but I agreed with him about Lenny. And so did his daughter Claire."

"Yes, Claire did all she could," the other woman said, "but with Lenny's mother and her own husband and her brother all working for Lenny, what could she do?"

"Willis Bulow would do anything his stepmother asked."

"Or anyone else, for that matter. His father kept him right under his thumb. I'll bet Willis shed no tears when Forrest died and he could call his soul his own."

"He'll never do that."

"You can't tell with that repressed sort. When they do break loose—"

"Willis break loose? That I'd like to see. If he'd been half the man Stan Tooling is—"

"Why Stan tried so hard to get Lenny free is one thing I'll never understand."

"The boys were always good friends, and Stan is a kindly soul."

"He'd be smart to remember that his wife has the money."

"I'll say for Stan that he never set out to get his hands on the Bulow money. Claire made a dead set for him."

"Ross Bentwick is back, too. At Ed Morison's. First time in years. Regular gathering of the clans."

"Queer, isn't it? Ross hasn't paid much attention to his uncle since he got to be a famous actor. Now he comes rushing back."

"At least, Ross never tried to get Lenny pardoned. Not that I ever heard of. Well, I ought to be getting along home."

"Oh, wait a little longer. They ought to come along any time now. The more of us the better. They may as well see right at the start we aren't giving Lenny any welcome. I wonder what it's going to be like, having a murderer living up here on the ridge?"

"And did you know Helen Quarles is coming back?"

"No!"

"Mr. Morison couldn't get anyone to rent her cottage so she has to take it herself."

"What's wrong with it, do you know?"

"Not for sure. People don't stay. You hear things but I don't know the straight of it."

"Doesn't your husband take care of the cottage?"

"Joe checks the oil burner and the water pipes and clears snow. But he told me—"

The storekeeper said, "Yes, ma'am?" and Paula was forced to wrest her attention from the gossiping women, buy some cigarettes and ask the way to Ed Morison's house.

He pointed it out to her and she turned to the left, down to the lower level of the old village and a beautiful white colonial house set in deep lawns shaded by oaks and maples. A tall gaunt woman with a plain face and the flat voice of Maine admitted her.

"You'll be Miss Savage," she said. "Your luggage came on the noon train and Mr. Ross brought it from the station."

She summed Paula up in a quick glance, approved of her, and led the way upstairs to a small but charming bedroom.

"There's some bigger rooms," she said, "but they were redecorated just this week and smell of paint. As soon as they are aired out, I'll move you."

"This is fine," Paula said and meant it. Compared with the room she'd been living in for months it was paradise.

"There's iced tea out on the back lawn where Mr. Morison is, when you are ready." The housekeeper took a quick look at the room and its adjoining bath and went downstairs.

As Paula walked across the lawn that stretched to the edge of a blue river lined with weeping willows, her feet made no sound. Two men were seated in canvas garden chairs with their backs to her. One of them had the actor's trained voice which carries easily. "Why didn't you tell me? You don't need this Savage woman. Let's fire her straight back to New York and I'll take over the research for you."

"The rôle of dutiful nephew doesn't suit you, Ross. A bit miscast. In any case, I prefer a collaborator who is reasonably sober."

"Perhaps you are right," the other said lightly. "But if that's not why you sent for me—"

"That's not why. I was—curious."

"I'll be clearing out tomorrow."

"I wouldn't do that if I were you," Morison said warningly. "It might make a bad impression when your boyhood friend Lenny Horgan has just come home. Don't you agree?"

Paula's face was burning. She could hardly turn around and go back to the house, nor could she raise her voice in a cheery greeting to stop this conversation. To her relief the bigger of the two men turned, caught sight of her, and came forward to meet her.

She recognized Ross Bentwick at once by the unmistakable way he carried himself. She had seen him cross a stage like that. He had a pleasantly ugly face, a strong jaw, prominent cheekbones, deep-socketed eyes, and every indication of a hangover.

"I am Paula Savage."

Ed Morison got up from his chair with difficulty, a gnome-like little man with an unexpectedly big bass voice.

"Thank you for coming, Miss Savage. I hope we can make you comfortable here. This is my nephew, Ross Bentwick." He had his nephew's harsh features and much of his nephew's intangible charm, but his face was marked by pain and tempered by a quality of serenity. He had come to terms with life.

"What on earth are you staring at, man?" he demanded.

Ross gave him a quick, amused smile. "You'll have only one guess." He turned back to Paula. "We've met before, haven't we," he said confidently. It was a statement, not a question.

"I think not," she said in the repressive tone that was usually successful in quelling male advances.

"Just the same, I am positive I've seen you somewhere. And I've heard your voice." He drew out a chair for her. "Will you have iced tea with my uncle or a highball with me?"

"Tea, please, and lots of ice. I don't need a drink."

He looked down at her, unsmiling, and poured a glass of iced tea. "You mean I don't need a drink. Won't you please tell me where we've met?"

"We haven't," she assured him crisply. "Of course, I've seen you. The last time was in *The Poisoner*."

The odd grimace made his mouth suddenly ugly and Paula became aware that Morison was watching his nephew with strained attention. Then he began to devote himself to Paula, chatting easily over a wide range of subjects.

It was she who brought the conversation around to the job. "You are planning to write a history of Coxbury, aren't you?"

"Or perhaps an epitaph. Epitaph for a dying civilization. You must have seen the stigmata as you drove up. It's a shock to see how little life-giving soil there is, how close the human race is to extermination without constant vigilance, to have the flood expose the sterile rocks like the bones of a skeleton."

Ross's eyebrows shot up. "I devoutly trust you aren't going to expose any skeletons. What are you planning to write—history or hearsay?"

"As Dr. Johnson remarked, 'If a man could say nothing against a character but what he can prove, history could not be written.' "

"I wonder what you are really up to," Ross commented.

His uncle's expression was sardonic. "So do a lot of people." He pulled himself to his feet and Ross reached for the cane that lay beside his chair. "Will you excuse me if I leave you for a while, Miss Savage? I've reached the age where I must have an afternoon nap."

Ross handed him his cane and then offered his arm. After a fractional hesitation, Morison accepted it and the two men walked slowly up to the house. Only then did it occur to Paula as queer that not a single reference had been made to the sudden and violent death of Helen Quarles.

II

Paula lay back in a garden chair, one hand on her lap, the other dangling over the side so that her fingertips rested in cool grass. She had forgotten there was peace like this and beauty and quiet that was broken only by bird song. If the job lasted long enough she might become whole again in this healing peace.

Peace! What a fool she was to have forgotten why she had come to Coxbury, why Mr. Potter had made her come against her better judgment. She wasn't here to dredge out facts for a local history. She was here to help find a murderer. Or rather, she reminded herself, since the identity of the murderer was known, to help send Lenny Horgan back to the penitentiary where he belonged, which he should never have left, and this time to the electric chair.

Though she had heard no one approach across the grass, she was aware that someone was behind her. Her nerves tightened and then she heard the soothing sound of a shaved ice in a cocktail shaker. She turned to see Ross Bentwick wielding a frosty silver shaker with one hand and holding two glasses with the other. He hooked his foot around a canvas chair and pulled it up so he could face her, handed her one of the glasses, gave the shaker a final swing and poured daiquiris into the two glasses.

Paula sipped hers, cold and tart. "Mm," she said appreciatively.

As he lifted his glass, Paula noticed his bloodshot eyes. Wasn't that what had gone wrong with his acting career? She had heard something; Bentwick was terrific but he wasn't reliable. He missed cues; worse than that, he missed performances.

He was watching her face and now he nodded as he raised his glass in a mock salute. "Othello's occupation's gone. Bentwick is on the skids. Or hadn't you heard?"

Perhaps it was the relaxation that made her speak her thought aloud. "Why are you?"

He grinned at her. "A wench after my own heart. Womanly concern. Shall I tell you the story of my life?"

"God forbid! And I'm not in the least concerned."

"But so virtuously disapproving!" He drained his glass and refilled it.

"Are you trying to quarrel with me?" she asked coolly.

He had the kind of face, she thought, that needed little make-up, the kind of head a sculptor would like to model, all pronounced planes. Seeing him at close range, she realized how little he had altered his appearance for the rôles she had seen him play, and yet his guilty doctor had given an impression of suave good looks and his Richard had been ugly and evil. His was the only Richard who had made convincing that fantastic love scene. He had repelled but he had fascinated the silly woman whose husband he had murdered.

"Quarrel with you?" He appeared to take the question seriously. "As a matter of fact—no. I'm just gathering a little Dutch courage before I go to see what twenty years in prison have done to Lenny Horgan. It's nothing I could take cold sober."

This was the opening she wanted. "I suppose you knew him well. What was he like?"

"Lenny was a kind of unfinished genius," he said slowly. "Or do I mean unfulfilled? He was brilliant in math. Years ahead of Willis or Stan or me. He didn't seem to work for it. It was just there like a flash of light. But one-sided. That was all he had. In other things, he was only average, and slower than most about people. Really stupid."

There was a kind of helpless anger in his voice. "Lenny never saw people as they were. And he wasn't ambitious. Queer—of the four of us I was the only one with ambition." His mouth twisted. "And look at me. Or perhaps you'd better not. But Lenny, with the best mind—there was no drive in him."

Remembering the vicious blow that had so nearly sent her plunging under the wheels of a taxicab, Paula said, "It takes some drive to commit murder."

"There you are. Virtuously disapproving."

"Most people disapprove of murder."

"I know. I know."

"After all," Paula was goaded by his mockery, "it's the worst crime there is."

In profile Ross's face was grim, but he spoke pleasantly. "That's where you are wrong. Dead wrong. There are a lot worse crimes but they are all safely within the law so they wouldn't disturb you much."

"Such as?"

"Such as cruelty, malice and all uncharitableness. Such as exploitation and domination. Such as sowing the seeds of hate and fear—or maybe those are the same thing. Such as cannibal mothers who eat their young and queen bee wives who destroy their mates."

Paula set her glass down carefully. Her hand was steady but her mouth was dry.

Ross seemed to be watching an agile little salamander but he said, "I appear to be saying all the wrong things today."

"What was wrong with that?"

"Damned if I know," he admitted, "but I flicked you on the raw." He ignored her protest, refilled her glass and put it in her hand. For a moment his fingers tightened their pressure on hers and then dropped away.

"What I am driving at," he told her, "is that the people who cause most of the trouble in the world remain unpunished—hell, sometimes we hail them as great men —but Lenny has paid with twenty years of his life for killing Evelyn Dwight."

"She paid with all of hers," Paula reminded him.

"And a damned good thing, too! Do you know what she would have done if she had lived? Injured everything she touched. There was no one she didn't hurt if she could—for the sheer pleasure of the thing."

"You make her sound like a monster," Paula protested.

"She was. But inside the law."

"Her picture—she looked so pretty—so sweet."

"She was pretty. And sweet—in a way. Very sweet. We boys called her the community chest. You can guess why. The innocent Evelyn initiated all of us." Ross laughed suddenly. "Except Willis."

He refilled his glass. "I'll tell you one thing, Paula Savage. There wasn't anyone who knew her well who wasn't glad to know she was dead. That's one reason why they were all so tough on Lenny."

"I don't see that."

"Don't you?" he said oddly. "You should see it. You have a lovely intelligent face. They had to punish Lenny for their own guilt. Because they wanted her dead. When she was strangled they were shocked at themselves and used Lenny as their—as their stand-in for punishment." Ross drained his glass again and emptied the last of the cocktails into it. "Nothing but ice water. I'll mix us some more."

She shook her head. "Not for me."

"No weaknesses at all, lady? I'll tell you what. Let's go see Lenny."

"Oh, no," she cried involuntarily.

"It's all right," Ross assured her. "Sylvia asked us. The more the merrier. Lenny needs support. He's going to have a hell of a time with his stepsister Claire. Probably with his step-brother's wife, too. After all, Ivy never met him until today and she can't be pleased at having an ex-convict in the family, let alone in the house with her. She probably expects to be murdered in her bed. Or she does if she has listened to dear Claire."

Ross's mouth twisted in a mocking smile. "You are bound to like Claire. Kindred spirits. She has no weaknesses either." He held out his hand and pulled her to her feet, staggering. "Come on, and let Claire Tooling be an awful warning to you."

The taunts of a drunken actor on the skids were of no importance, no importance at all, Paula assured herself. Anyhow, it was obvious that, with the obstinacy of the drunk, Ross Bentwick intended to pay a call on Lenny Horgan and he was unfit to drive.

"All right," she agreed. "Provided I do the driving."

III

Paula surveyed herself dubiously in the mirror. She looked keyed up. She closed her eyes, made her body relax, from the tense jaw to the tips of her fingers. She took a long breath.

Try not to think that you're going to meet a murderer. Maybe your own murderer. The curtain is going up and you'll step out of the wings, one of those casual entrances that take you across the stage at an oblique angle like an Agnes DeMille ballet, half turned away from the audience. A society comedy with a Coward touch. They'll need that to balance Lenny's presence. Very light and bright and brittle. Now!

She opened her eyes and was satisfied with what she saw. "You'll do," she said and went down to join Ross, taking her handbag and car keys.

As he climbed in beside her, he pointed out the two big houses on the upper road, a huge gray stone and a sprawling green ranch house. "The stone house was Forrest Bulow's. He built it up there so he could look down on Uncle Ed. Uncle Ed gave him a start and Forrest never forgave him for it. Forrest was a very unforgiving man. A punishing man. A jealous god. He always reminded me of the guy in Browning's 'My Last Duchess,' who put his wife to death because she smiled at other people. Just smiled, mind you! Claire is like her father. Forrest wanted his domination to show." Ross laughed. "That's what infuriated him with his second wife. Sylvia is as soft and elastic as a pillow, with the temperament of Jello. Nothing Forrest ever could do made a lasting impression on her.

"The ranch house next door is Willis's, and that is as far as he ever got from his father during the old man's lifetime. We are going there."

As Paula turned into the big circular parking space before the ranch house, Ross said, "I seem to have a talking jag. I must be high as a kite."

"You are," Paula assured him.

"That's the little woman. Running true to form. Are you a descendant of Carrie Nation?"

"No," Paula snapped, "but right now I wish I had her ax."

"It wasn't an ax, it was a hatchet. You are thinking of Lizzie Borden."

Paula realized that it would be unwise to continue the quarrel with Ross in his condition. He had reached the unpredictable, irresponsible stage of drunkenness. She said mockingly, "I wonder that you will still be talking, Signior Benedick; nobody marks you."

"What, my dear lady Disdain! Are you yet—" Ross broke off. "Got it! Beatrice. I knew I'd seen you somewhere. *Much Ado about Nothing.* The programs were gone so I never knew your name."

The door was opened by a young woman with a narrow vivid face and a vivacious manner.

"Hello, Ivy. Miss Savage—Mrs. Willis Bulow."

Ivy welcomed Paula with a smile and drew her into the room where she introduced her to her husband's stepmother, Mrs. Forrest Bulow, a monstrously fat woman, who took up most of a love seat and sat nibbling salted nuts, beaming at everyone; to her sister-in-law, Mrs. Stanley Tooling, smart and attractive except for a jaw like a spade, who gave her a sharp scrutiny, a perfunctory handshake and then ignored her; to Stanley Tooling, a pleasant, round-faced man who brought her a drink and slapped Ross Bentwick on the back, greeting him with loud outcries. Stan, like a salmon hurling itself upstream, was attempting the hard way to inject a festive note into the gathering.

The cocktail party seemed to Paula to fall into a series of isolated tableaux, probably because it never jelled into a successful whole. Most of them were trying too hard. Claire Tooling wasn't trying at all. Paula wondered if it was her doing that the small table at which Lenny Horgan sat under a pool of light playing chess with Willis Bulow was isolated from the rest of the group, whose chairs had been drawn together in a rough semicircle.

Paula's breathing was uneven as Ivy, smiling brightly, led her to the table where the two men were playing chess. They got up to greet her. Willis Bulow, a slight man with small neat features, his eyes concealed by dark glasses, bowed without speaking. Lenny Horgan, stout, balding, middle-aged, gave her a faint apologetic smile and murmured something indistinct.

Paula smiled vaguely while she looked at the man who had tried to kill her, who might try again. At the moment he did not seem to be interested in her. He stood looking at Ross. Then, wordlessly, the two men clasped hands.

"Well, you old horse thief," Stan said to Ross, "it is months since I've seen you. We'll have to get together and plan things. Remember the fun the four of us used to have, raising hell?" His voice faded out as though he were aware of his lack of tact. He lifted his glass. "To the future."

Glasses were raised but he was unable to generate any heat.

Unexpectedly, it was Lenny who broke the awkward silence. He had a quiet voice, which he seemed unaccustomed to using. "Don't try so hard, Stan. We can't pretend the past isn't there."

"We can forget it," Stan insisted.

"Speaking of forgetting," Ross put in, "I forgot to bring back those Casals festival records of yours, Ivy, though Uncle Ed told me to be sure—"

Lenny moved a piece and looked round with that curious sidelong glance of his. "Do you still do that? Exchange books and records and magazines?"

"Oh, Ross," Claire said sharply, "my house is simply overflowing with your theatrical magazines. I don't know what to do with them."

"Throw them out."

"But there are some articles about you."

"There won't be any more." Ross stumbled against a table and set a lamp rocking.

Stan caught the lamp and for the first time became aware of Ross's condition. "Sure there will," he said jovially.

Ross grinned wolfishly at Paula. "You tell him, Beatrice. You tell him, my lady Disdain. Which reminds me —why don't you act any more? What are you doing among the skeletons of Coxbury?"

Stan touched his arm and led him away. At the same

moment Claire said, "Miss Savage, I understand that you are employed by Mr. Morison to help with his book, that Miss Quarles unearthed you for him. Do tell me how she is. It is so long since I have seen her."

Paula was caught off balance. "Why—she—" She looked around the room for help and saw, with a little shock, that Lenny was watching her. "She seemed very well. Of course, I'd never met her before."

Claire raised her brows. "How odd! I assumed that she would have to know something about your background and all that before recommending you."

Paula was aware that her color was rising but she kept her temper. Ivy Bulow gave her sister-in-law a curious look and said lightly, "If your Miss Quarles isn't exceptionally stupid, she could tell at a glance that Mr. Morison would be frightfully lucky to have Miss Savage. Isn't it a pretty drive up here from New York?"

"Very pretty." Paula looked down at the chessboard. "That reminds me. On my way up today, or rather on the outskirts of Coxbury, I passed an antique shop that had the most amusing chessmen I've ever seen, a hand-carved Chinese set; all the pieces were little men playing the game, looking puzzled or intent or self-satisfied. One of them was signaling a move behind his back. It was the gayest set!"

Lenny's face lighted up. "That sounds like fun."

His mother's eyes thanked Paula. "An antique shop? There are so many in Connecticut. It's practically a major industry. Do you remember which one?"

"There was no name but you couldn't miss it. A converted red barn with a sign: 'Antiques—Good and Bad.' "

"My favorite antique shop sign," Ivy put in eagerly, trying to keep the conversation on safe ground, "was 'Trash bought—treasures sold.' I always thought it rather disarming."

Willis pushed back his chair. "This man is fabulous. I know when I am outclassed." It was the first time Paula had heard him speak.

"You get more like Uriah Heep every day," his sister remarked contemptuously, "except that you don't wriggle. But you grovel enough." She turned to Lenny with such vindictiveness in her face that Ross hastily switched on the radio to check what she was about to say.

At the same moment Stan exclaimed, "Hey, Willis, I've been doing all the work. How about you slaving over a hot stove for a change and freshening our drinks?" He gave a warning glance at Ross to indicate that he had passed his quota. "Lenny, will you mix your own?"

There was a queer little smile on Lenny's lips. "You'll have to do it. I don't know how. When I was—sent up— I was too young to drink."

Stan looked at him speechlessly.

Paula wondered if anyone else was aware of the way the four men automatically ran interference for each other.

The radio came on with a roar of static and Ross reduced the volume.

". . . no end of the heat wave in sight. The temperature at four o'clock was 96 degrees, the humidity 88%. A news bulletin just in states that Helen Quarles, who was killed in Central Park last night, has been identified as the key witness in the notorious Horgan murder trial of twenty years ago."

There was the faintest possible pause and then the newscaster went on smoothly, "It is doubtless a coincidence that Lenny Horgan was released from prison yesterday. In signing his pardon, the Governor said that the unswerving faith in Horgan shown by his family and devoted friends during the years while they worked for his release gives him hope that the future will prove to be a fresh page on which will at last be recorded the achievements of a mind that, at one time, gave evidence of exceptional qualities. The Governor denied that his action in granting the pardon was influenced by the heavy financial backing and the political power wielded in the state by—"

Ross managed at last to switch off the radio, to silence the voice that so cautiously, so deviously, made its deadly points.

He began to laugh discordantly. "Here we go again!"

Seven

There was no one at the breakfast table as Paula went into the big sun-flooded dining room where only one place had been set. The housekeeper came in with orange juice in a bowl of chopped ice and a pot of coffee.

"Am I too early?" Paula asked. "No one told me."

"No, I'm the one who is late. Mr. Morison being so sick in the night and all, I overslept. Would you prefer eggs or waffles?"

"A waffle, please. Is Mr. Morison ill?"

"He had a heart attack last night. After he heard that radio broadcast about Miss Quarles. It's not too serious but the doctor said to stay in bed. The only way he can keep Mr. Morison there is to have nurses in the house to watch him. There's one upstairs now, getting him cleaned up for the day."

Paula's heart sank. "Then, perhaps," she said, "it would be better if I go back to New York."

The housekeeper shook her head. "Mr. Morison was most particular about it. He wants you to stay. The only trouble is that with Mr. Ross in his old room and the other guest rooms still smelling so strong of paint, we've got to put the nurse in your room. Mr. Morison thought if you wouldn't mind taking Miss Quarles's cottage—it's a real cute little house, whatever they say—it would only be for a few days, likely, and you'd have your meals here—"

"Of course. I'll pack at once."

"Just what you'll need for the night. There's no rush. I'll run over myself this morning and make up a bed and air the place out. Mr. Ross will take your suitcase." She added, "If he ever gets up. He's still sleeping it off."

"Libel," Ross declared from the doorway. "Got some black coffee? Uncle Ed not down yet?"

The housekeeper told him about his uncle's attack.

"How serious is it?" he asked sharply. "Why didn't you call me, Florence?"

The housekeeper gave him a disillusioned look. "You wouldn't have waked if they had sounded the last trump."

While Ross drank his coffee (black) Paula noticed that his eyes were more bloodshot than ever, that his hand had a pronounced tremor. He looked up swiftly, catching her eye before she could look away.

She was prepared for a renewal of hostilities so she was surprised when he said, "I'm sorry about yesterday. Drunk and disorderly. I got off to a bad start with you. Do you think we could begin all over again?"

"It wasn't important," she said lightly.

"I'm not sure that's the way I want you to take it." For a moment he looked at her intently, then he seemed to forget her altogether. "Why in the name of all that's holy," he burst out, "did that newscaster hint that Lenny killed Helen Quarles?"

"After all," Paula pointed out, "she testified against him. She sent him to prison."

"Oh, sure, but—"

"And he hated her for it."

"Rot!" Ross said rudely. "Lenny didn't blame her. You don't know the first thing about Lenny if you think—" His eyes narrowed. "Just what did that woman tell you?"

"She only talked about the job."

"Like hell she did! You are lying your head off, Paula Savage, but have it your own way. Come on."

"Where?" she asked in surprise.

"Uncle Ed won't want you this morning. Let's go find that chess set you were describing last night and get it for Lenny. We owe him something. Or won't you trust my driving? Oops! There I go again. My bad genius makes me say all the wrong things to you."

"Does it matter?"

"Yes," he told her frowning, "I think it does. Please come."

He took his own car, a long rakish two-seater, and drove like a demon. Paula held on grimly, keeping her eyes off the speedometer. His attention was fully occupied and he made no attempt to talk, for which she was grateful. Anyhow, she was trying to remember Mr. Potter's description of the antique shop. If she shouldn't be able to find it—but she saw the sign, "Antiques—Good and Bad," and pointed it out to Ross.

In a vegetable stand beside the road there were two oil paintings, which a blond young man was examining. He glanced at Paula and away without recognition. The smaller of the two canvases represented a dirt road with a pool of water just after the rain had stopped; the other was a long panel showing a narrow band of gleaming river when the light had almost faded and the land was dark. In the background a tall chimney stood alone.

Ross sat looking at them for a long time. "I suppose," he said at length, "no self-respecting collector buys representational art any more but, my God, how that fellow brings home the fact that light is your only painter."

As he got up to open the door for Paula, a big Pontiac station wagon drove up beside them. Willis Bulow was at the wheel and Lenny Horgan was beside him.

Ross waved cheerfully. "Take a look at those canvases! They're terrific."

The two men came over to inspect the paintings, nodding to Paula, Willis casually, Lenny shyly.

"I like more color and brightness," Lenny said in a diffident way. "These pictures are too dark for me."

Willis looked at them for a moment; then he said sharply, "I hate amateur art. Connecticut is infested with it in summer. It's bad enough to have the place cluttered with exhibits but when they put the stuff out on the highway—flaunt it—let's go look at that chess set, Lenny."

The blond young man turned to look interestedly at Willis's darkened face.

A tall man came out of the barn to greet them. "Good morning, can I help you?"

"Yesterday," Paula told him, "you had a Chinese chess set. May we see it?"

"I'm afraid you are too late. I've just sold it to this gentleman." He nodded to the hovering blond man.

Ross shrugged. "Well, that's that."

Paula turned to the purchaser. "Would you mind very much letting us see it? I tried to describe the little chess players but—"

"Not at all. It hasn't been packed yet. Come take a look."

They trooped into the barn where, on a table near the double doors the chessmen had been set out. Lenny bent over, examining the pieces one by one, chuckling with delight at the wit with which they had been conceived.

"Perhaps," Willis said, lowering his voice, "you might consider selling the set to me as my stepbrother likes it so much. Any reasonable price—"

"I've been hunting this particular set for a long time. Sheer luck I ran across it here. But perhaps—would your stepbrother care to play a game with me? My name is Potter. I've got all the time in the world. I'm vacationing. Just drifting around."

Willis hesitated. Then he introduced himself. "This is my stepbrother, Lenny Horgan."

There was no expression on Mr. Potter's face. He spoke to Lenny who answered in his quiet voice. Neither man offered his hand. Mr. Potter repeated his invitation.

"Can we play here?" he asked Kurt.

"Sure. There are a couple of chairs you can use if you dust them off. But sit down easy, will you? They are rickety, like all this junk. Glad to have you. It will provide a touch of Montmartre. Add admosphere to the joint."

"Speaking of atmosphere," Ross put in, "who did those oils?"

"I did, but I didn't put them on display. That was my wife's idea."

"Then they aren't for sale?"

Kurt was stunned. "My God, do you want to buy one?"

Ross laughed and the two men strolled over to the vegetable stand. Willis and Lenny were discussing whether Willis should wait for Lenny or come back for him. Paula drifted toward Mr. Potter.

"Good work," he said softly.

"I've got to talk to you," she told him.

"Pick up anything?" Mr. Potter went on smoothly, "Personally, I can't pass an antique shop without picking up something."

Paula turned to see Ross watching her, cold fury in his face.

"I should have known! The way you dragged that chess set into the conversation yesterday, it was too damned pat. Pretty work, my lady Disdain. Pays better than acting, I suppose." Ross turned on his heel and went out to his car. The motor started with a roar and he shot off.

"Lady," Kurt said plaintively, "here I catch a potential buyer at a weak moment and you drive him away."

With a murmured apology for Ross's rudeness, Willis offered Paula a lift home. After Ross's driving, which was based on the simple principle that a car should be forced to its top speed, Paula was prepared to relax with Willis at the wheel. Willis, she thought, was not a man to break speed limits. She was right about that but wrong about the relaxation. Ross had been the master of his car at seventy-five miles an hour; Willis was the slave of his at thirty-five. He gripped the wheel as though afraid the monster would get away from him, he sounded his horn at every turn, he braked whenever a car passed in the opposite direction, he watched in alarm the traffic behind as though expecting it to crash into him.

"I hope," Willis said in that slightly phony British accent, "you will make allowances for Ross. He is upset about Lenny and it just hit him that way. Ross takes understanding. We've known him all his life and they don't come better. It is hard, under the circumstances, for any of us to be quite normal, especially since Miss Quarles's —death. You were a close friend of hers, weren't you?"

The question had slid in so casually that Paula was un-prepared for it. No, she said, she had met Miss Quarles only once. Willis turned to look at her, the car swerved and he straightened it with a jerk.

"What did she tell you, Miss Savage?"

"We talked principally about the job."

"Oh, come," Willis said good humoredly, though there was no good humor in his face, "it's absurd to think she would talk about Coxbury and not mention—any of us."

As the car coughed, he exclaimed in dismay, "We're out of gas!"

There was a filling station across the road. When the attendant had adjusted the nozzle of the hose he came up to put one grease-blackened hand on the open window.

"Look, Mister, it's none of my business, see, but I'll give you a friendly tip. Get that guy Horgan out of Cox-bury. People didn't like his coming back in the first place; but now he—now Miss Quarles got herself killed, there's going to be real trouble."

"This is an outrage," Willis declared.

The attendant shrugged. "Okay. It's no skin off my nose, one way or the other. Like I said, just a friendly tip." As the car pulled away from the pump he watched, impas-sive.

"God!" Willis exploded. "This is horrible. What are we going to do? If Lenny can't make a place for himself here, where can he go?"

As a woman waved, he braked without warning and the driver of the car behind, who had missed him by inch-es, swore at him as he swung around to pass.

The door was opened and Ivy Bulow climbed in, drop-ping a large paper bag on the seat beside her.

"Thank heaven, I saw you! These groceries are so heavy I couldn't have managed much longer. Hello, Miss Savage. Isn't this a divine day?"

Paula observed that, for all the fixed bright smile, the determined gaiety of manner, Ivy looked pale and drawn.

"Why didn't you tell me you planned to shop?" her husband asked. "I'd never have let you walk."

"I didn't plan to. Intended to order by telephone as I always have. But they refused to deliver."

"Isn't Friday their regular day?"

"You don't understand, darling. They won't deliver at all. Not to us. It was awful. They didn't say anything. They just—the storekeeper and the customers—they stared at me. They were so terribly silent. They hate us."

"Look here, Ivy—"

"Willis, I'm frightened. Something awful is going to happen."

Eight

Molly Jepson looked after an overloaded Ford car in wonder. "What makes people do it?"

Her husband grinned at her. "If we sell the stuff we shouldn't complain because people buy it."

"But that horrible chair. Big and ugly and uncomfortable. What do you suppose they'll do with it?"

Kurt pulled out his billfold. "And the washbowl, pitcher and thundermug with the red roses. And the cracked mirror. And the table with the wobbly legs. Sixty-nine clams we've made out of that deal."

"It hardly seems honest." Molly touched her husband's arm. "What are we going to do about that?"

He followed her eyes to the two men who sat in silent absorption over the chessboard.

"I'm guessing," he said, his voice low. "We have to play it by ear. But I figure we are supposed to maintain this French café atmosphere. You might drift over and ask if they would like some grilled cheese sandwiches and beer."

Her hand tightened on his arm. "He's a murderer." Her voice was almost soundless.

He put his arm around her. "If Potter suggests playing here, it's all right. He'd never let you in for anything."

"Hi," Molly called, "we're having cheese sandwiches and beer. Will you join us?"

"That will be fine." Mr. Potter raised his head to smile approvingly at her and she knew that Kurt had been right.

Lenny hesitated. "Do you know who I am?"

Mr. Potter looked down at the wreckage of his carefully planned game. "One of the world's best chess players," he answered truthfully. He leaned back and lighted a cigarette, after offering his case to Lenny.

No one could play chess with Lenny and fail to be impressed. He played a brilliant game and a bold one. He also moved faster than anyone Mr. Potter had ever encountered. There seemed to be no hesitation at all. The whole thing might as well have been laid out before him on a chart. Mr. Potter said so in disgust.

"Well, it is in a way," Lenny said apologetically, as though he had no right to play so well. "That is, it seems so logical, so easy. I've never understood why people think there is any thing difficult about it. After all, chess is only a game."

Mr. Potter was silent, trying to balance the bold and brilliant playing against the timid and apologetic man. The ex-convict was made up of fascinating contradictions: the broad intellectual forehead and the indeterminate mouth; the plump, rather flabby face that had aged without maturing and the eyes behind the steel-rimmed glasses that were old and spent.

Kurt came down the outside stairs and brought them each a grilled cheese sandwich and mugs of beer. He studied the board and grinned.

"You'll need a little reinforcement," he told Mr. Potter cheerfully, "after the beating you have taken." He eyed Lenny with respect and sketched a mock salute. Before going inside he said, "Hey, if you see any more suckers looking at the stuff and making like customers, give me a shout, will you?"

"Suppose I scare them away?"

"If this junk doesn't, you won't," Kurt assured him.

Mr. Potter raised his mug. "Cheers."

Lenny picked up his own. "I shouldn't be here," he said uneasily. "They wouldn't be feeding me if they knew who I am."

Shock treatment, Mr. Potter decided, was the best method of handling him. "Oh, don't be an ass! The Jepsons know who you are. Everyone around here knows who you are. A man who has come back to rebuild his life. Stop looking over your shoulder."

Lenny lifted his mug and drank deeply, trying to cover his confusion, though he could not hide the color that had risen in his pasty face.

"Yes, I suppose they do. Notorious character and all that." He smiled wryly. "You know, that's a queer thing to think about yourself. It seems as though you mean some other fellow. It always has seemed like that, as though it were some other fellow."

He looked shyly at Mr. Potter who had attacked his sandwich. "You are very easy to talk to. This is the first time I've felt like saying anything about it." He picked up his sandwich and put it down again. "Funny, when I was—in prison—I thought a lot about decent food, but now I don't seem to be hungry. It's all so different. Being outside, I mean. Not the way I expected."

He took a sip of the beer. "I don't mean I hadn't realized there would be changes. I just didn't take in the fact that you can never return to the place you have left. You aren't the same, the place isn't the same, the people—"

He put down the beer mug and his fingers tightened around the handle until the knuckles were white. "Mr. Potter, what is going to happen to me?"

Mr. Potter saw the panic in the young-old eyes.

"Miss Quarles was killed. You heard?"

Mr. Potter nodded.

"God," Lenny said, "they'll think I did it. Ross was right. Here we go again. But to live through it twice—"

"Steady there," Mr. Potter said. "In the first place, no such claim has been made. In the second—"

Lenny shook his head. "This time they don't need to put me on trial for murder," he said shrewdly. "A few hints, like the one on the radio last night, and I'll be convicted in the eyes of the public. And you know damned well that counts. It will mean I'm finished. I should never have come back to Coxbury. All along I knew it would be bad for my mother, that it would make Claire tougher on her."

He smiled and for the first time Mr. Potter found him

likable, caught a glimmering of the charm he was reputed to have had as a boy.

"Of course, to be honest, it's just as tough on Claire. She's so ambitious and here comes an ex-convict stepbrother. It's hard on Willis's wife, too, but not as bad as it is for Claire. Ivy feels more secure; she's never had the *nouveau riche* uncertainty, that vulgar longing for the 'right people.' And then, she's so in love with Willis that she is glad to do something hard for him."

He talked with a child's naïveté, as though assuming that Mr. Potter knew the people who made up his private world, and the latter made no comment, simply gave a comprehending nod from time to time.

"You know," Lenny went on, "I'd never have thought of Willis as the man to inspire a passionate love; so far as I can see, he doesn't even know it is there. I could never figure Willis out or get close to him, though all the time I was in prison he came to see me once a month. Never missed. And he worked like hell to have me pardoned."

Lenny picked up one of the tiny chess players and turned it around in his fingers. "And now, after forty-eight hours of freedom, I seem to be headed back, and this time to the chair."

"Use your head on this, Horgan," Mr. Potter said quietly. "Instead of panicking, try to think it out. As I said, there's no murder charge yet. But suppose the worst; you can certainly produce an alibi for your first night out of prison."

Lenny's laughter betrayed how close he was to panic. "Then get a load of this. My mother had permission to take me to New York for the night to escape reporters. She borrowed a friend's apartment. We got there and all of a sudden it really hit me that I was free. I couldn't bear to be penned indoors. So I took a walk. Alone. I walked down Riverside Drive and along Broadway and Fifth Avenue and I—"

His voice was steady but there were fine beads of perspiration on his forehead. "I walked home through Central Park. Nice, isn't it?"

He saw the consternation in Mr. Potter's face and laughed again.

Mr. Potter pushed back his chair. "Cut it out," he said sharply. "You've been under a strain and you've had a shock, but this is no time to let go. Let's take a ride somewhere."

Lenny did not move, though he had checked the laughter that threatened to get out of control, that was edged with hysteria. "What concern is this of yours?"

Mr. Potter grinned at him. "It's about time you started cultivating a little healthy distrust and looking at people's motives as though they were gold bricks. That is bad advice to give most people because, as a rule, there is too much distrust floating around. But you—good God, man, you're the original fall guy!"

He was so indignant that Lenny laughed again and this time the laughter was genuine, unstrained. "You're quite a character, Potter." Without warning he thrust out the chessman. "That yours?"

"Yes."

"Did you find it here at this junk shop of the Jepsons?"

"No," Mr. Potter told him blandly.

Lenny thought back. "That beautiful girl—Miss Savage—the one who told us about the set—you put her up to it? That was bait to get me here, wasn't it?"

Mr. Potter nodded.

"Ross figured that one out. That's why he was so sore at her. Ross was always a loyal friend." Lenny was watching Mr. Potter. "He is a very loyal friend," he insisted.

"I haven't denied it," Mr. Potter said mildly. "But there's one thing I am damned sure of. One of these people isn't your loyal friend."

"I don't know what you are driving at. What are you after? Why did you come to Coxbury?"

"I came here," Mr. Potter told him pleasantly, "to prevent you from murdering Paula Savage."

II

The Volkswagen was parked off the road in the shade of a clump of weeping willows. The two men had tramped for miles along the river, walking aimlessly. Now and then, Lenny paused to point out an old landmark or to indicate changes caused by the flood. They rounded a bend in the river and saw a chimney standing alone in a field.

"What in the world?" Lenny began. "Oh, that's where the picnic shack was. The flood must have washed away everything except the chimney. How queer it looks. Why, that's the chimney in Jepson's picture back there, the one Willis hated so."

"It must have unpleasant associations for him."

"Perhaps. Mine are pleasant enough. Some of the happiest times I ever had. We used to come here as kids, bring a picnic basket, go swimming and fishing and canoeing. Stan and Claire and Ross, Willis and Evelyn and me. And at night we'd build a big roaring fire."

"Night picnics?"

"Oh, no." Lenny was amused. "Daytime and properly chaperoned. Either mother or Miss Quarles always came along. But at night I came here with Evelyn now and then, when Miss Quarles was asleep and she could slip away from the cottage. It was a natural place for kids to make love. I wasn't the only boy, and Evelyn wasn't the only girl. Just one of those things, I guess. Miss Quarles would have had a fit."

His tone changed. "You know, Potter, I can't take all this in, that someone killed her and tried to kill Miss Savage. No matter what Miss Quarles may have told her, there was no conceivable reason—" He always referred to her as Miss Quarles. The schoolboy respect for his elders was so drilled into him that it never occurred to him to mention her in any other way.

"I never hated her. From the moment I killed Evelyn I knew I'd be punished. I never expected any different, and I never blamed Miss Quarles for testifying. If you had seen her in court, she felt so bad about it—I never hated her."

"But someone," Mr. Potter said patiently—he had been pointing out the fact for the past hour—"told her that you hated her. Someone warned her repeatedly that you would make her pay for it if you ever got out. Who did that?"

Lenny shook his head.

"You aren't thinking, Horgan," Mr. Potter said irritably, "and you've got to think. Whoever fed Miss Quarles this story must have convinced her that they got it at first hand. How many people have been in touch with you?"

"My mother, Stan Tooling, and my stepbrother Willis Bulow. My mother came to see me every week, the others every month."

"Who else?"

"No one."

"How about Ross Bentwick?"

"No," Lenny said slowly, "Ross didn't come." He propped his hip against a boulder and stood looking at the ground. "You know, one thing occurs to me. You are thinking about the people who were in touch with me, instead of the ones who were in touch with Miss Quarles, and they aren't the same people. She went abroad right after the trial and she wrote only once to my mother. She never corresponded with Willis or Stan or Ross. There were only two people who were in constant touch with her: Mr. Morison and my stepsister Claire."

He took off the steel-rimmed glasses to polish them and Mr. Potter observed again how defenseless his eyes were.

"What are you trying to prove?" Lenny asked. "That no one but me could have killed Miss Quarles?"

"Right now," Mr. Potter told him, "I am trying to figure out who lied to her—and why. I'd like to know who telephoned to her night before last."

There was startled hope, but a very tentative hope, in Lenny's face. "You don't think I killed her?"

"No," Mr. Potter admitted in some surprise. "Damned if I do!"

"Well—well, that's fine," Lenny said lamely. "But then —what is this all about?"

"I think it grew out of the murder of Evelyn Dwight. Why did you kill her, Horgan?"

"To protect my mother."

As Mr. Potter looked at him speechlessly, Lenny explained, "To understand that, you'd have to understand my mother's second husband. Claire is like him. Dominating. Not imaginative. Tenacious about what belongs to her. Forrest Bulow never cared much about Willis. He browbeat him and humiliated him and kept him under his thumb. He didn't like me at all. Whenever I got off the rails he took it out on my mother. He was a man who had to punish."

Lenny hesitated, trying to shape his thoughts, and especially his feelings, in words. "He frightened people. He controlled them by frightening them. And he was possessive. Take Willis, for instance. He never liked Willis, but he wouldn't let him go. And he had a dog once that ran away to the people next door. He—killed him."

Lenny shut his eyes as though shutting out some ugly picture in his mind.

"Well, I'd fallen for Evelyn. All of us did. She was as pretty a girl as I ever saw. We boys were only sixteen and Evelyn was two years older and a hell of a lot more experienced than any of us." He grinned. "Ask Willis about that. Anyhow, when we got in pretty deep she— changed. She began to threaten us."

"Threatened to tell about your relations with her?" Mr. Potter asked.

"Oh, no. Other things. She must have been one of the youngest blackmailers who ever flourished and she was successful, too. We were all handing over our allowances and pilfering more at home for her. We even got to stealing cars and selling them to a guy who drifted into town and paid us cash. He must have had dozens of kids like us all over New England doing his dirty work for him."

Mr. Potter was interested. "What happened to him, do you know?"

Lenny shook his head.

"Was he ever mentioned at the trial?"

"No one but the four of us ever guessed he had any part in the car stealing—at least, so far as I know."

"Which of you was approached by the man in the first place?"

Lenny shook his head again. "I can't remember now. I don't even recall what he looked like, except that he was tall and thin. His name—uh—I think we called him Mossback but I don't know why. Some sort of nickname, I suppose."

"Well, to get back to Evelyn. What did she use for pressure?"

"I don't know what she had on the other boys," Lenny told him. "With me it was my mother. That night, I took Evelyn to the movies and when I bought the tickets she saw I had only a couple of dollars left. She told me she had to have twenty dollars right away or she would tell my stepfather that my mother was having an affair with Mr. Morison."

Lenny added slowly, "I couldn't let that happen to my mother and I knew nothing would stop Evelyn, so I killed her."

"But, good God, man, you aren't making sense!"

"More sense than you'd think. You see, I knew Ed Morison had begged my mother to leave Forrest; he wanted to take care of her. And she wanted to do it. But she was afraid. Forrest would never have let her go. And I thought of the dog—just because the neighbors were kind to it—and Forrest took out his revolver and shot it through the head. Not in a rage. Like an executioner."

Lenny saw the look of incredulity on Mr. Potter's face. "I knew him," he said stubbornly. "But I can't see what that has to do with this mess now, with Miss Quarles's murder and the attempt to kill Miss Savage."

"I think I am beginning to see the connection," Mr. Potter told him. "I have a feeling that you were tricked

deliberately, that someone hoped to get you so stirred up
about Evelyn Dwight that you'd scare her into putting an
end to her blackmailing. Only it backfired. You went
farther than anyone could have anticipated."

"That's fantastic."

"Someone," Mr. Potter said, "used you for his own
purposes. I agree that the thing is fantastic and it is ugly.
God, it is ugly. And that, I think, is what Miss Quarles
guessed. But there are a lot of things that have to be explained."

"Name some."

"Well, to begin with, Miss Quarles couldn't rent her
cottage because it was ransacked every summer. It's a
cinch you didn't do that. I want to know who was searching that house and what he was looking for. I want to
know what pressure Evelyn Dwight brought to bear on
Ross and Willis and Stan. I want to know how many people wanted Evelyn silenced. Because one of them sparked
her murder. Find who that was and we'll know who broke
Helen Quarles's neck, night before last."

Nine

In response to Paula's tap at the door, Morison called, "Come in," in his big deep voice. Ross, who had been sitting beside the bed, got up as she entered the room. He pulled a chair forward for her without speaking, and Paula knew that he was still angry.

"I'm awfully sorry to be uprooting you this way, Miss Savage," Morison said.

He seemed very small propped against the pillows. His lips were almost blue and his skin had a gray cast. It sagged around the jaw and lay in folds on his neck. In a few hours he had aged greatly and Paula felt a momentary stab of pity. How vulnerable the old are! And then she saw the steady eyes that made no demand on her sympathy, that required none, and realized that only Morison's body was vulnerable. His mind was tough enough to see him through anything that might be in store for him.

"The whole thing is a pack of nonsense," he said. "Doctor's orders. But I'll fire the nurse in a few days and you can come back. Meanwhile, you won't be too uncomfortable at Helen's cottage. One thing you can count on. I won't expect all your time. Like Thoreau, I love a broad margin in my life. So I want you to enjoy yourself as much as you can."

Ross gave a short bark of laughter. "I'll leave this beautiful friendship to ripen."

His uncle stopped him before he reached the door. "Just a minute, Ross. I haven't had a chance to ask how Sylvia is taking that libelous broadcast last night, linking Lenny with Helen Quarles's murder."

"She was stunned, as we all were, but Sylvia is an amazingly resilient woman."

"You mean," his uncle said tartly, "that you think she has no feelings."

"They certainly," Ross commented, "have not made her appetite less—exuberant."

"In some ways," Morison said, "you're an awful fool. Did you ever hear of compensatory eating? Comic, isn't it? Not as pathetic as growing thin and fading away. One of nature's ungenerous tricks. Sylvia was beautiful—my God, but she was beautiful!—and Lenny's sentence destroyed her life as surely as it destroyed his. She blamed herself, heaven knows why, and she changed. She began to eat as though food were her sole reason for existence. She became terribly overweight, she destroyed her own beauty. And if that seems hilariously funny to you—"

"It doesn't," Ross said quietly. "Please don't get so stirred up, Uncle Ed. It's bad for you. Try not to worry."

Morison snorted. "If there is a more infuriating piece of advice than that I don't know what it is. We've got to find a way out of this intolerable situation. Here's Lenny in an impossible spot."

"Damnable," Ross agreed.

"I want to help him. I've loved Sylvia all my life and there's nothing I ever had that she wanted—excuse that touch of bathos—but at least I can help her son."

As Paula got up, he said, "Sorry to involve you in these family affairs, Miss Savage."

"She doesn't mind," Ross assured him. "I know that before long we'll all be regarding her as one of us."

"If you can put up with me and my graceless nephew, I'd like you to stay," Morison told her.

Reluctantly, Paula resumed her seat. Ross's open mockery was not as bothersome as the older man's manner. She had the uncomfortable feeling that she was being used, that she was being maneuvered in some way.

"What I have in mind," Morison said, "is this. Reason I wired for you to come home, as a matter of fact. Forrest didn't leave Lenny a cent and Sylvia has only a life income. Whatever lies ahead for Lenny is going to be tough. I'd like to divide what I have: half to you, half to

Lenny. After inheritance taxes, you'd each have enough to live on. Of course, you would be the loser, but—"

For a moment, uncle and nephew looked searchingly at each other. Then Ross said lightly, "Why not?" He groped for the knob as though his vision were clouded. Then he opened the door and went out.

Morison looked shrunken, almost as though he had lost weight overnight. "You've seen my nephew on the stage, haven't you?" he asked abruptly and Paula remembered Miss Quarles telling her how devoted he was to the nephew who had been a bitter disappointment. She had the curious impression that the conversation she had just heard had been a test of some sort, a test that Ross had failed to meet.

"Oh, yes. I've seen him several times."

Was he good? Mr. Morison didn't, he told her, want to be put off with tact. He wanted the truth.

"He's exceptionally good," Paula assured him. "Brilliant, as a matter of fact. He doesn't play a part, he lives it. And he has an astonishing technique; not a wasted motion, not an inflection of the voice that doesn't add to the characterization. And yet—"

"Well?"

"He's generous," Paula said slowly. "With his terrific personality he could easily steal every scene; as though Heifitz were first fiddler in a quartet."

"But he lets you hear the whole quartet," Morison said, greatly pleased.

Paula nodded.

"Then what went wrong with his career?"

"I don't know," she admitted. "There were rumors that he drank too much to be reliable."

Morison let out his breath in a mirthless snort. "You don't need to tell me Ross drinks. I can see that for myself." He looked over her shoulder. "Come in, Stan."

"Hello, Mr. Morison. Afternoon, Miss Savage." For once Stan Tooling's round face was not smiling. The eyes he turned on Paula were anything but friendly and she realized he had heard Morison's comment and thought she was trying to undermine Ross with his uncle.

"I'm heavy with messages," Stan told them. "Claire's love, Mr. Morison, and she is awfully sorry to hear of your attack and please let her know if there is anything she can do. And a message for you, Miss Savage. Claire wants everyone at our place for a cook-out tonight. A kind of gathering of the clans to show we are all squarely behind Lenny."

"That was Claire's idea?" Morison said incredulously, hitching himself higher on his pillows.

Stan was momentarily uncomfortable. "Well, the cook-out is her idea, the gathering of the clans is mine. We've all got to put our wits together and clear up this mess. All right with you, Miss Savage?" There was a faint edge on his voice. "Shall I have Ross bring you along?"

Paula flushed. "As a stranger—"

"Frankly," Stan admitted, "that's why I am putting the heat on you. The presence of an outsider tends to keep things smoother, don't you think?"

When Paula went downstairs she found that Ross had piled her luggage in the back of her car and his two-seater was parked in front of it.

"I'll lead the way," he said, "and you can drive your own car, so you'll have it when you need it."

He leaned on the door of her car. "Stan tells me you've been having a nice heart-to-heart with Uncle Ed." He grinned. "You're getting to be practically one of the family, aren't you? I'm to take you to the Toolings tonight. That ought to provide material for a meaty article on Home Life of a Murderer."

"I'm not a reporter," Paula told him hotly. "I—did—not—come—here—for—a—story." The words were widely spaced for emphasis.

Ross surveyed her coolly. "All right, I'll buy that. But what are you up to? I'm still right about you using that chess set as bait to get Lenny to your friend."

"I mentioned the chess set because the conversation was awkward and I thought any change of subject would be helpful."

Ross shook his head. "I'm not buying that. Claire was asking you about Helen Quarles. What was so awkward about that?"

"I knew she was dead. I'd seen it in the morning paper. So—"

Ross's eyes had narrowed. "So you jumped to conclusions. You thought Lenny had killed her."

"Well, I wondered," Paula admitted. "I couldn't help wondering."

"What in hell had the woman said to make you think that?"

Paula wished that he would stop leaning over the window of the car, that he would remove that unswerving gaze and release her. "She was afraid to come back," she said.

Ross whistled. "Well, I'll be damned."

II

"This is the place," Lenny said.

Mr. Potter turned into the circular parking space and looked at the rambling ranch house. The door opened and a fat woman came lumbering out to the car.

"Lenny!" she exclaimed. "I was worried when Willis said he had left you behind. I was afraid—" She broke off to acknowledge his introduction to Mr. Potter. "Do come in," she said warmly, and led the way into a room that was nearly all glass.

"What's wrong?" Lenny asked his mother.

"That beastly broadcast last night. We're going almost crazy. Reporters on the telephone and even at the door. We are practically in a state of siege. That's how I happened to see you drive up. We've decided not to answer the door unless we know who is there."

"I'll have to go away somewhere," Lenny said. "That's the only way to put a stop to this."

"You aren't going one step!"

Something in Sylvia's tone brought Mr. Potter's eyes quickly to her face. Phlegmatic as she looked, she could become a tigress in defense of her young. Seeing her as she was now, it seemed incredible that this woman had attracted two husbands and, apparently, a lover. He wondered if she had ever guessed her son's motive for the crime that had deprived a young girl of her life and had made a hell of twenty years of his own.

It occurred to him that no one had as strong a motive as Sylvia Horgan Bulow for desiring the death of Evelyn Dwight. If any suspicion of her affair had reached her husband, he would have been a formidable enemy. But on whom would his punishment have fallen: on Sylvia herself or on the man she loved?

Mr. Potter took a firm hold on his wayward imagination. The theory he had been building was that Helen Quarles had been killed because she knew the identity of the person who, in her own words, had put Lenny up to murder, a person whose position was so vulnerable that he could not risk exposure even now.

But unless two people were involved, which he considered unlikely, it was improbable that Sylvia herself had killed Helen Quarles. She could have done so—yes. She was big and the Quarles woman had been slight and frail; also, it was understandable that even a timid woman would not have hesitated to meet the woman who had been her dearest friend.

And yet, though the crime had been designed to pass for a mugging, there had all along been the likelihood that Lenny, who was in New York, would be accused. If Sylvia had intended to kill Helen Quarles, Mr. Potter felt sure she would have provided her son with an unbreakable alibi.

"I'll ask Ed what to do," she said. "Ed will know. Ed always knows." She broke off as the telephone began to ring and eyed it warily, as though it were a wild beast that might spring at her.

Willis came in to answer the telephone. As he listened, his expression changed, his lips compressed, his skin began to darken with rage as it had done during that curious episode at the red barn when he had seen Kurt's painting of the stone chimney. Mr. Potter wished that the man would remove his dark glasses.

As Willis put down the telephone, Ivy Bulow appeared in the doorway. "Who was it?"

"Just a crackpot. He wanted—he said Lenny has to leave the village, that the people are stirred up."

"He's not to go!" Ivy exclaimed. "People are beastly. Cowardly. They ought to be ashamed to hound and threaten like this."

"If only Ed weren't ill," Sylvia lamented, "he could handle it. People always listen to Ed."

Ivy looked questioningly at Mr. Potter and Lenny performed the introductions. Mr. Potter, he said, had been giving him a game of chess.

Ivy smiled radiantly as she held out her hand. "How nice that Lenny has found a fellow enthusiast! I do hope you'll come often to play with him. We are all duffers at the game. Potter? Not Hiram Potter? Then I've met you before, at the big party Glen and Blair Forbes gave on their first wedding anniversary. I stayed on after the crowd left and Glen drank a special toast to you. He said he owed it all to Hiram Potter."

Mr. Potter laughed. "You make me sound like a marriage broker."

Ivy laughed too. "He said you saved him from a murder charge when he was caught up in that Bluebeard horror."

Willis wheeled stiffly. "Are we to understand that you are a detective, Mr. Potter?"

"No," Mr. Potter told him sadly, "I just meddle."

Sylvia said impulsively, "Will you meddle with this, Mr. Potter? Because I'm afraid things are getting out of hand."

"Sometimes," Mr. Potter told her, "people regret asking me to meddle."

Her magnificent black eyes studied him shrewdly. "I can believe that."

Willis cleared his throat. "Sylvia darling," he said, with a deprecating laugh, "don't you think it is rather unfair to involve Mr. Potter in our private concerns? And—

injudicious to do anything that might—worsen the situation? The most well-meaning intentions, as I am sure Mr. Potter's are—"

"My dear Willis," Sylvia expostulated, "must you sound so stuffy? Something has to be done and if Mr. Potter would have the great kindness—"

Mr. Potter looked from face to face. "I am," he confessed, "an insatiably curious man. An unsolved puzzle torments me. Not an attractive character trait, but there it is. But before I go any farther there is one point I think you should all understand. Someone killed Miss Quarles. Her neck was broken not because she was a passing stranger attacked by a mugger but because she was Helen Quarles."

"I suppose you have some evidence of that," Willis said coldly.

"I have plain common sense and a slight knowledge of Miss Quarles. She was a timid woman. She would never have gone alone into Central Park at night. She would never have gone with a stranger. The only people she knew in America lived here in Coxbury."

Sylvia nodded her head. "Oh, yes," she said flatly. "I've been coming to that conclusion all day. One of us killed her. All right, Mr. Potter. Cry havoc."

Willis turned and went quietly out of the room. Ivy stood looking after him, with one hand pressed to her mouth. Then she turned to face Mr. Potter. Her head was high but she was very pale.

"We are going to the Toolings for a cook-out. Do join us, Mr. Potter. Claire will be delighted to have you." She smiled but there was a touch of defiance in her manner. "You'll have an opportunity to look us all over."

III

The cook-out was being held on the patio behind the gray stone house. A man in a high chef's hat grilled steaks over charcoal and a trim maid was laying out a buffet table with salads, casseroles and hot breads, while Stan rolled a portable bar across the lawn to the guests seated at the table.

Ivy performed the introductions and Stan shook hands with Mr. Potter almost eagerly to offset the chill in his wife's manner when Lenny appeared. Claire was unexpectedly gracious to her uninvited guest but Mr. Potter was aware that he owed his welcome to the fact of Ivy's sponsorship. Claire, he observed, was impressed by her sister-in-law.

He ambled away to look at a carefully tended rose bed and consider the people at leisure. Claire was the dominant personality of the group. But for all her assured manner and her spadelike jaw she was, he thought, uncertain. She was keeping a sharp eye on the two servants, anxious that everything should be done properly. There was a kind of deference in her manner toward Ivy who, with Stan, was working without apparent effort, to keep the talk flowing easily.

Willis was proving to be of little assistance. He took a daiquiri from the portable bar and withdrew to one of the little tables. Sylvia reached for some salted almonds on the buffet table and munched solemnly as she went over to join her stepson. They exchanged a few low-pitched remarks, a question by Willis, a reply by Sylvia. Then they fell silent but Mr. Potter was aware that she was watching him and he was somberly watching his wife.

Ivy slipped her hand under Lenny's arm and drew him toward Mr. Potter. "I was wondering," she said in a low tone, "do we tell the others about you?"

"You must do as you like."

"I think I'd rather wait," she admitted. "There's no advantage in getting Claire stirred up, is there?"

"You think Mrs. Tooling would object to my interference?"

"Not interference," Ivy said gently. "Intervention. And we are most grateful."

"I hope," Mr. Potter said soberly, "you'll have no occasion to change your mind."

"Hi, there, Ross!" Stan called cheerfully. "Good evening, Miss Savage. How nice of you to come."

Mr. Potter watched Paula walking toward them, thinking again how beautifully she moved. Tonight, there was more than an illusion of beauty, she was really beautiful, in a green knitted dress with a matching cardigan. The other women paled beside her; even Ivy's vivid quality lost its vitality and seemed muted.

Claire turned to Paula. "I believe it should be Mrs. Savage."

Paula stopped so short that Ross nearly bumped into her. "Yes," she said evenly, "it is Mrs. Savage."

"You should have told me last night." Claire smiled blandly. "Then I wouldn't have gone on speaking as though you were an unmarried woman. Or—I believe you are a widow, aren't you?"

"Yes," Paula said stiffly.

"Such a tragedy," Claire went on. "So sad for you. And not really knowing how it happened makes it so much worse."

"But I know how it happened," Paula said through stiff lips.

"Oh, yes, you were there, weren't you?"

Claire slipped her hand under Ross's arm and drew him away, rather pointedly leaving Paula alone. Stan wheeled his bar beside her, poured her a daiquiri and asked how she liked her steak cooked.

"Who," Claire asked Ross, "is Ivy's boy friend?"

Ross followed her eyes and saw Mr. Potter. "Ivy's friend!" he said in surprise. "I thought—"

Claire called in the voice that she meant to be cordial and that sounded peremptory, "Mr. Potter, I don't believe you know Mr. Bentwick."

The two men nodded to each other and Mr. Potter joined them.

"How did the chess game come out?" Ross asked.

"He took my skin off," Mr. Potter admitted.

Afterwards, he looked back on the evening as one of

the most unpleasant he had ever spent. Claire appeared to have set herself the not uncongenial task of making the situation untenable for Lenny and Paula. Ivy and Stan were finding it uphill work to maintain a normal atmosphere. Willis, silent and withdrawn, made no effort. Sylvia sat watching them all, her huge black eyes moving somberly from face to face.

She is looking for a murderer, Mr. Potter thought, and what a choice: her stepson, her stepdaughter, the latter's husband, and the nephew of the man she loved.

Stan circulated cocktails assiduously until the steaks were served and afterwards kept highballs moving. Little by little, the tensions relaxed as the voices rose. The only one who consistently refused the highballs was Ross Bentwick. It was Ross, finally, who put the party on its feet.

Stan broke into one of Claire's bitter tirades about the reporters by asking Ross to do his imitation of a cub reporter interviewing a politician's bride.

Ross started to refuse and unexpectedly agreed, doing sketch after sketch. They were witty, acutely observed, and side-splittingly funny. The onlookers laughed until they were helpless, until they held their aching sides and wiped tears from their eyes.

And in the exhausted quiet that followed, Paula spoke, her voice unexpectedly loud in the silence and shockingly thick and blurred. "When you can act like that, ish a pity to be bitter dish—dishappointment to your uncle, as Miss Quarles said."

They stared at her, too taken aback to do anything.

"Miss Quarles?" Willis said, startled.

Paula nodded solemnly and her head went on nodding like a mechanical toy. "She told me about all of you; she told me everything." There was a little pause and then she said clearly, her voice not blurred at all, "That's why she was afraid."

Claire said in a tone of disgust, "Good heavens, the woman is drunk!"

"I brought her," Ross said, "I'll take her home." He

laughed. "My dear lady Disdain! Who'd have thought it?"

Beside the other man Mr. Potter was slight of build, but he moved Ross to one side without difficulty. "She is going with me," he said.

Ten

"I never was so surprised in my life," Claire said. "I didn't suspect a thing and then, all of a sudden, I realized she was dead drunk. And yet I don't know why I was so surprised."

Ross grinned. "Come on, Claire. You know you are dying to tell us. That 'Mrs. Savage' line. Where did you get it?"

"From one of your own theatrical magazines. Before throwing them out, I thought I might as well look at them. Somebody ought to get some good out of them when you paid for them. Well, it turns out she is an actress and her husband is dead. He was shot."

Stan was thunderstruck. "You mean he was murdered?"

"Well, the inquest made it suicide, but I guess people didn't think so. Anyhow, there was a terrible scene and some woman called her a murderess and she just—vanished after that. Then she turns up here. Drunk. Stan, how much did you give her to drink?"

Stan made a bewildered gesture. "No more than the rest of you. Of course, I left the bar over there so you could help yourselves. I didn't watch it. I'm terribly sorry, Claire. I shouldn't have asked a woman we didn't know anything about."

Claire shrugged. "Ross, you'll have to warn Mr. Morison about her tomorrow. We certainly can't have her here and the way we're all in and out of each other's houses, it will be an impossible situation. Anyhow, a man with heart trouble shouldn't have a drunk around him. You never know what they will do."

"Anyone can have too much to drink once in his life," Ross said. "What bothers me is that we let her go home in that condition with this fellow Potter. We don't know anything about the man and it isn't the kind of thing you leave to a stranger."

"He's a friend of Ivy's," Claire said.

"Don't worry about the girl, Ross," Ivy said reassuringly. "She'll be perfectly safe with Mr. Potter."

"I'm not worried about her," Ross said irritably. "I just felt it was an odd thing to do, that's all."

"He moved so darned fast," Stan said in chagrin. "He had her on her feet and halfway across the lawn before I realized what he was up to. I couldn't very well grab her away from him. I'll go around in the morning and make sure she is all right."

"My own opinion, for what it is worth," Claire put in tartly, "is that it isn't the first time she's been drunk."

"I doubt that," Sylvia said. "Helen Quarles recommended her. Helen must have known her very well to have talked so freely about all of us."

"Helen didn't know anything about us, anything that all Coxbury didn't know," Willis said.

"Didn't she?" Sylvia said almost indifferently, but her eyes continued to move in that tireless search from one familiar face to another, seeking something unfamiliar.

"This Savage woman is a trouble-maker," Claire said crisply. "If Ross doesn't do something about her, I'll see Mr. Morison myself. All we need at this point is to have someone spread scandal around the village. In a way, though, I am glad Mr. Potter took her home. This is no time to have strangers in the house. We've got to decide what to do."

She turned swiftly to Lenny. "Let's be honest about this. You've simply got to go away. You are ruining everything for me—for all of us—here."

"Wait, Claire," Stan protested.

"Don't try to stop me," she snapped. "You and Willis have always been soft in the head about Lenny. You got him out of prison and you'll live to regret it. But I say he ought to go away and let us alone. He's done us enough harm."

"Look here, Claire," Willis began.

"Oh, Claire, don't—" Ross said at the same time.

"Stop, Claire!" Sylvia's voice, without being raised, silenced both men. It silenced Claire, too. "We've done Lenny more harm than he has done us."

"Not I!"

Sylvia looked at her stepdaughter and the latter's eyes fell. "I could make out a pretty good case. Don't try me too far. And understand this: Lenny is not going to leave Coxbury. If he did, he'd never have a chance to come back again. We are going to fight it out here and now."

"And let Lenny kill someone else?" Claire broke off with a cry as Stan's hand cracked hard on her cheek. "Stan, you hit me," she said unbelievingly.

"Sorry, darling. I didn't know how else to stop you."

"And now," Sylvia said coldly, "I'll tell you something for your own good, Claire. I've asked Mr. Potter to help us. He has helped other people who have been in great trouble, other people who have been involved with murder. Because I won't permit Lenny to be victimized."

"But someone killed Helen Quarles," Claire said stubbornly.

"Yes," Sylvia said heavily, "someone killed her. Deliberately. She was lured to Central Park by someone she trusted and the only people she knew were here in Coxbury. She was killed by one of us, Claire!"

"You're out of your mind," Claire choked. "No one but Lenny had a reason."

"I suppose," Sylvia said, "we all had reasons, when it comes down to that. But unless I'm very much mistaken, Mr. Potter will find out what they are."

"Is that a threat?" Claire asked.

"It's a warning," Sylvia told her.

"What's wrong with everyone?" Claire cried. "Stan—"

He put his arms around her. Over her head his eyes signaled and the others went quietly away across the lawn.

When they had gone, Stan patted his wife's shaking shoulders.

"You hit me," she sobbed. "You hit me in front of them all. You hit me."

"I'm sorry," he whispered. "Terribly sorry. But you must not say things like that, say that Lenny would kill someone else. Let him alone."

"Then get him away from here," Claire said. "Do you hear me? Get him away from here. He's not going to destroy what I have built. Nobody is going to destroy it."

He kissed her wet cheek. "Nobody is going to destroy it," he promised her.

"Stan?"

"Yes?"

"It was Lenny who killed her, wasn't it? It couldn't be proved—Sylvia was lying—it wasn't one of us." She clung to him. "I'm afraid," she whimpered. "I'm afraid."

He tipped back her head, trying to see her eyes. "Why," he demanded urgently. "For God's sake, tell me the truth. What are you afraid of?"

II

"Well," Ross said cheerfully, "I've wanted to slap Claire for years. More power to Stan. I thought she had him cowed."

"I wish he hadn't done that," Lenny said uneasily. "It was on my account. It will only get him in bad with Claire."

"Don't worry about her," Ross advised him. He was sprawled out in one of Ivy's low chairs, smoking.

Lenny switched out the lights. "I like the dark. Up—there—the lights burned all night."

They sat in silence and in darkness, watching fireflies flash their lanterns on and off among the bushes on the lawn.

"Queer about that girl getting drunk," Lenny said.

"There's a lot about Paula Savage that is queer," Ross agreed. "Not to speak of her highly checkered past or the mysteriously defunct husband."

"It's a pity she drinks. She's so lovely to look at. And her voice is so delightful I like hearing her talk, no matter what she says. Ross, do you think Miss Quarles told her—"

"The way Potter hustled her out, he wasn't taking any chances on her letting us know what she might have been told," Ross commented.

"Mr. Potter doesn't miss any tricks," Lenny was surprisingly cheerful.

Ross tried to see his face in the darkness but could make out only the dim outlines of his body sitting bolt upright in a chair by the window. "What's the lowdown on Potter?" he asked. "What is Sylvia up to? That crack about one of us killing Helen Quarles—what, in God's name, is going on?"

"Potter's idea is that someone primed Evelyn with that —story she told me—knowing that I would try to find some way to scare her so she'd quit threatening all of us. He thinks Miss Quarles guessed who did it. He thinks—"

"So that's it." Ross was startled. He stared into the dark, thinking furiously. "So that's it," he repeated oddly. "Well, at least, we know what we are up against. But just what in hell we are going to do—" He switched the conversation. "When are we going fishing?"

"It depends on how long I can stay here."

"You'll stay. Best thing you could do. And I want you to try out my new car. A hundred and thirty m.p.h. on a good road, and handles like a toy."

Lenny laughed. "I couldn't drive anything like that. It's twenty years since I've been behind the wheel of a car. I don't understand the new ones. I'd never be able to hold it on the road."

"Sure you could," Ross insisted. "Nothing to it."

They were silent for a long time and then Lenny spoke out of the darkness. "Ross, why couldn't Miss Quarles rent her cottage?"

"I haven't the slightest idea. What brought that up?"

"Oh, I got to wondering about it," Lenny said. "I wonder about a lot of things. What did Evelyn have on you?"

Ross hesitated. "She was going to tell Uncle Ed I had raped her. Get him to disinherit me."

After a pause Ross spoke tentatively. "Lenny?"

"Huh?"

"I suppose you wonder why I never went up to the prison to see you."

"Oh, that's all right," Lenny said uncomfortably. "No reason why you should. And I knew you'd have hated it more than the others. You have more imagination."

"I couldn't go," Ross said bluntly.

"Yes," Lenny told him. "I understood that, too."

III

Willis was standing at the window staring out into the night when Ivy went into his room. She closed the door and stood beside him, slipping her hand under his arm. He had removed the dark glasses but even so his eyes were bleak, his face remained closed against her.

"Ivy, what do you know about this man Potter?"

"He is a friend of Glen Forbes, a wealthy man who is fascinated by mysteries. He saved Glen from arrest in that Bluebeard case. Glen thinks he is wonderful."

"I still can't see why Sylvia wants him to meddle in our affairs."

Quick color came into Ivy's face at his tone, a spark of anger showed in her green eyes. She jammed her hands deep in the pockets of her housecoat.

"Look here, Willis," she said evenly, "I think it is time we clear up a lot of things. We're not merely drifting along, we are drifting away from each other. I can't reach you at all. We've got to be honest, no matter how difficult it is. Anything is better than living with this wall between us. When we were first married, I made myself a promise that I would never invade your privacy, never try to force your confidence. But I was wrong. We are turning into distrustful strangers."

"Distrustful?" he said slowly. "I've never distrusted you. Never. What you mean is that you distrust me."

"Is it trust," she asked, "to shut yourself away from me like this? Can't you tell me what is wrong?"

He grunted impatiently. "Can't you see for yourself what is wrong? The whole place is ganging up on Lenny."

She shook her head. "Not now. Not since Mr. Potter came into the picture. One of us may be headed for trouble, yes, but not Lenny."

"One of us," he said slowly. "Claire, Stan, Ross—me. Are you sure we want to know which one of us it is?"

"Yes," Ivy told him.

"Whatever happens?"

"Whatever happens," Ivy said. "And whatever happens, I love you, Willis. Completely. Irrevocably." She put her arms around his neck and Willis pulled her violently against him. "Ivy! Ivy!" he choked. He took off her housecoat and lifted her in his arms.

A long time later Ivy turned her head sleepily against his shoulder. "Darling—the night Miss Quarles was killed —where were you?" When he made no answer she said, wide awake now, "You weren't in the apartment. I looked."

"Why?"

"Because," she turned to kiss him, "I had to look for you because it was so long since you had come looking for me. I had begun to wonder—"

"Do you wonder now?"

"Not about that. But—where were you?"

Eleven

Mr. Potter bent anxiously over the girl who was slumped on the seat beside him. Her mouth was partly open, her breathing was heavy. Then he started the car and drove down to the lower level of the old village. He drew up before the Morison house. After he had rung several times, bolts were pushed back and the door was opened by the housekeeper, wrapped in a dark woollen robe, her hair covered by a heavy net.

He told her that Miss Savage had been taken ill and found all his tact called upon to prevent her from rushing out to the Volkswagen to see for herself. She explained that Miss Savage had been moved temporarily to Miss Quarles's cottage and told him how to get there.

No, she said in answer to his question, there was no telephone in the cottage but he could use the one in Mr. Morison's library.

While she planted herself firmly beside the telephone, determined not to be defrauded of her rights, he called the doctor and urged him to come immediately to the Quarles cottage. Then he dialed the Jepsons' number.

"Kurt," he said, aware of the woman who listened avidly, "will you and Molly please go at once to Miss Quarles's cottage, prepared to spend the night? Miss Savage has been taken ill and she needs a woman with her. You'll have my heartfelt gratitude."

He escaped as well as he could from the housekeeper's questions and ran back to the car. Paula's head had fallen forward and her breathing was slower, more laborious.

Miss Quarles's cottage was not hard to find, a neat white Cape Cod. It was around a bend in the road and out of sight of any other dwelling, though it was only a couple of hundred yards away from the nearest house.

No wonder it had been possible to ransack the place. Mr. Potter found the doorkey in Paula's handbag, unlocked the door, turned on lights and ran back.

He lifted Paula out of the car, half carried and half dragged her into the house. There was nothing bigger than a love seat in the small living room so he hoisted her upstairs, guiding her stumbling feet, urging her on. Of the three bedrooms only one was ready for occupancy. He laid Paula on the bed and bent over her. He lifted her lids and looked at her eyes.

Then he ran downstairs, filled a tea kettle and ransacked cupboards. He found a jar of instant coffee, left by some former tenant, and spooned it lavishly into a cup. As soon as the water was hot he dissolved the coffee and took it upstairs.

With considerable effort he got the girl to swallow some coffee and set her on her feet. "You've got to keep walking," he told her. "Come on now. I'll help you." He heard a car, let her sink down on the bed and went downstairs. A Buick had pulled in behind his car and a heavy-set man with iron-gray hair came toward him, carrying a small black bag.

"Dr. Graves? I am Hiram Potter. This way." He took him upstairs to the bedroom where Paula had fallen asleep.

"This is my patient?" The doctor drew back from the fumes of rum. "Drunk! Why didn't you tell me that over the phone?"

"Most of the rum has been spilled on her dress. I'm afraid she has been drugged, but I didn't care to explain that over the telephone."

With a muttered exclamation the doctor bent over the unconscious girl.

"So far as I can make out," he said after a pause, "she's in fairly good shape. Of course, I don't know how much of the stuff she has had. It's some barbiturate. You'd better tell me what you know about this."

When Mr. Potter had finished, he glanced at the doctor and sighed. "You know," he suggested, "you might be able to rid your mind of any misconceptions about me if you check with Captain Foote of the Connecticut State Police. We were involved in a queer case together last year and he'll be able to assure you of my good faith."

"I'll do that when I leave here," the doctor said. "Damned right I will. For a stranger to come into this village and try to tell me that one of our leading citizens —a Morison, a Bulow or a Tooling—tried to kill this woman is more, frankly, than I can stomach. If there was any hanky-panky, Lenny Horgan was back of it."

"No one tried to kill Miss Savage tonight," Mr. Potter said, "though an attack has been made on her life in the past forty-eight hours. This, I think, was simply an attempt to discredit her, to make her appear drunk, to force Mr. Morison to get rid of her. Someone is scared as hell of what Paula Savage might have heard from Helen Quarles. Believe me, Doctor, Lenny Horgan isn't responsible for this."

The doctor gave him a measuring look. "Just what do you suspect?"

"I think one of the people at the Toolings' tonight was responsible, indirectly perhaps but still morally responsible, for Lenny killing Evelyn Dwight. I think Helen Quarles guessed who it was and had to be silenced when she was forced by a diminished income, to return to Coxbury. I think that the person who killed her also tried to kill Paula Savage, believing Miss Quarles had passed on the information, and now is trying to discredit her so that, if she does talk, what she says won't carry any weight."

A car door banged. "We don't want anyone around," the doctor said.

"Friends of mine. Discreet and reliable. I thought there ought to be a woman with Miss Savage."

Mr. Potter ran down to open the door for the Jepsons.

"What is all this?" Kurt began. "I don't like to drag Molly into—"

Mr. Potter silenced him and took them both into the kitchen. While he made more coffee he rapidly sketched the situation.

"Well, I still don't like it." Kurt was angry. "I'll help you in any way I can but I'm not going to let Molly get mixed up with a thing like this. I'll take her home and then—"

"Nonsense," Molly said. "Give me the coffee, Hiram, and I'll see what can be done. You pour oil on my troubled husband."

When Mr. Potter had soothed his ruffled friend, he went upstairs. To his amusement Dr. Graves had succumbed to Molly.

"Stay out," the doctor told him brusquely. "Mrs. Jepson will help. We'll call if we need you."

After an appalled glance at the doctor's preparations to deal with the situation, Mr. Potter retired with relief and joined Kurt who, after a disgusted look at the love seat had settled himself in the larger of two very small armchairs, with his long legs stretched out on an ottoman.

"Molly all right?" he demanded with a scowl.

"Florence Nightingale herself," Mr. Potter assured him. "I am damned sorry to drag you two into this unpleasantness but I didn't know what else to do."

Unpleasant seemed to be an inadequate word for the sounds that came from upstairs.

"What's up anyhow? Has your convict friend broken loose again?"

Mr. Potter shook his head. So far as he could see, Lenny Horgan was the only one in the clear.

"Then who pulled this trick?"

Mr. Potter shrugged his shoulders. "You pays your money and you takes your choice. Here are the people who could have drugged her tonight: Lenny Horgan, Sylvia Bulow, Willis Bulow, Ivy Bulow, Claire Tooling, Stan Tooling, Ross Bentwick. We can eliminate Ivy Horgan. She never met Willis until six years ago and she never saw Helen Quarles in her life. And I think we can eliminate Sylvia Bulow."

Kurt shifted his position. "So you are left with Willis, Claire, Claire's husband and Ross Bentwick. Any favorites?"

"Claire," Mr. Potter said promptly. "The only drawback is that I have no more reason to suspect her than any of the others. I simply happen to dislike her intensely. She is doing her damnedest to drive Lenny out of Coxbury and she was obviously gunning for Paula Savage. She had her in target range long before the firing started. Then, too, Claire is the one who corresponded with Miss Quarles all these years, the one in the strongest position to have warned her about Lenny. In fact, only two people could have done that: Claire Tooling and Mr. Morison. And there's another factor. Claire is the only one who dislikes her stepmother; it would have been like her to tell Evelyn that story about Sylvia and Mr. Morison."

Kurt grunted. "You don't suppose Claire could be protecting her husband, do you? According to village gossip, she really hooked that lad."

"She might be, though I doubt if Claire would back anyone who was headed for trouble."

"There's a lot of talk about Morison's nephew," Kurt said. "He seems to be a bit of a bad egg. The idea is that he is sucking up to the old man for his money and that Morison has had a bellyful."

"Somehow," Mr. Potter said slowly, "I doubt if Morison would give Bentwick house room for more than five minutes if he were involved in this business. Morison was in love with Lenny's mother. Actually, that is why Lenny killed the girl, to keep her from telling Bulow that his wife was having an affair with Morison."

"That's a rotten lie! Not a word of truth in it!"

At the savage anger in Dr. Graves's voice the two men turned to see him standing in the doorway, glaring at them. Mr. Potter performed the introductions. The doctor nodded curtly to Jepson and faced Mr. Potter.

"Where did you get hold of that filth?"

"Lenny Horgan," Mr. Potter told him quietly.

The doctor blinked his astonishment. "But it's preposterous. There is no truth in it. None whatever. Ed Morison always loved Sylvia. He never made any bones about it. She could have married him any time in the past thirty years. She still could, for that matter. But though she has the warmest affection and the greatest admiration for him, she was never in love with him in her life.

"And aside from that, Sylvia wouldn't cheat. And Ed—my God, that man is the soul of honor. I can't see him making love to another man's wife. Neither of them is the kind to snatch at happiness, to grab what isn't freely and openly theirs, to get what they want at the expense of someone else's pain. And have no doubt about it; Forrest Bulow wasn't my favorite character but he loved Sylvia as much as it was in him to love anyone. Who planted that infamous story with Lenny?"

"It was more indirect than that," Mr. Potter explained. "The story came through Evelyn. Someone primed her, expecting her to use it in her own inimitable and attractive way. She appears to have been a flourishing young blackmailer."

"Perhaps," Kurt suggested, "it was someone who was jealous of Lenny and wanted to get rid of both Lenny and Evelyn at the same time."

"You mean Willis," the doctor said shrewdly. "But Willis has worked like a stevedore to get Lenny pardoned."

Mr. Potter looked keenly at the doctor. "You think Willis had more reason than the others for hating Evelyn." It was not a question.

The doctor shrugged, hesitated. "I shouldn't be telling you this," he admitted. "I learned it from Willis years after Evelyn died. He was deeply upset, in a disturbed condition that worried me at the time and I had to get at the root of the trouble. It seems Evelyn made a point of initiating the Coxbury boys in sex and when it came to Willis, he—well, he fumbled it. Evelyn did a swell job of ridiculing and humiliating him with his failure and Willis, who was too much of a lone wolf anyhow, didn't realize that he wasn't the first one it ever happened to. It set up a kind of psychological block; took him a long time to get over it. Add that experience to Bulow's ruthless ways of dominating the boy, holding him back, and it's a wonder to me he's not a lot more dangerously repressed than he is."

Kurt hunched up his shoulders in distaste. "I feel as though I had wandered into one of those damned Eugene O'Neill plays. This community is getting me down. And that reminds me, Potter. If you are so hell-bent on solving mysteries, you can solve one for me. Somebody slashed one of my canvases to ribbons. A poor thing, perhaps, but mine own." He spoke lightly but Mr. Potter knew that he was badly shaken.

"Not that long panel of the river?"

Kurt nodded. "How did you know? Damn it, don't look so pleased."

"I'm awfully sorry," Mr. Potter told him. "I think it's the best thing you've done. It's a damned outrage." But in spite of his words, he looked highly contented.

"Then why are you smirking like that?" Kurt demanded.

"Well, you see, things are beginning to happen at last."

II

By two o'clock the cottage had settled down. The doctor had gone home, after an odd speculative look at Mr. Potter. Molly was asleep on the other twin bed in Paula's room. Kurt Jepson, after putting his car in Miss Quarles's garage beside Paula's, and running the Volkswagen off the road behind a clump of bushes, had stretched out on an unmade bed in the room across the hall from his wife.

Mr. Potter sat in the dark in the small living room, recalling with self-distaste how fatuously he had assured Paula that he would be on hand to look after her. She had been drugged before his eyes and the contents of most of a glass of rum had been spilled on her dress. But when and how had it happened?

Whoever had doped her naturally hoped to get her away before anyone discovered it was not alcohol that was responsible for her behavior. Ross Bentwick was the one who had attempted to take her home. Ross was one of the boys who had been blackmailed by Evelyn. Would Morison have disinherited him if he had known about the car-stealing deal? Would he disinherit him now if he were aware that Ross had paved the way for Evelyn's murder and ruined Lenny's life and his mother's? Judging by what he had heard of Morison, there was little doubt that Ross Bentwick stood to lose a great deal. He had a reputation for drunkenness but he had been the only one to refuse highballs during the evening. It would be interesting to learn why he had taken such uncharacteristic pains to remain sober.

It would also be interesting to learn what had gone wrong with Bentwick's career. After seeing his performance during the evening, Mr. Potter was aware that here was a man of exceptional talent.

Willis? So far as Mr. Potter could recall, he had not spent any time alone with Paula. He could have doped her drink but, so far as that was concerned, so could any of them. And Willis was the only one of the lot who had been drinking rum.

Mr. Potter considered the case of Willis Bulow. His connection with the car stealing provided a sound reason for wanting Evelyn out of the way. Forrest Bulow's punishment would have been prompt and drastic. And he had hated the girl because of his personal humiliation, which appeared to have left a permanent scar that was entirely incommensurate with its importance. On the other hand, he could have no reason for desiring Miss Quarles's death. His father was dead, his inheritance was secure. His wife, surprisingly enough, adored him and would stand by even if his part in Evelyn's murder were to be revealed.

So? Mr. Potter remembered the dark rage that had struck Willis when he had seen Kurt's painting of the stone chimney, that reminder of the place where he had met Evelyn. Apparently Willis could be a violent man if he were aroused. And yet he had worked, as the doctor said, like a stevedore to get Lenny free from prison. Friendship or conscience?

Stanley Tooling? Certainly, it would have been easiest for him to dope her drink. He, too, had been involved with Evelyn and the car stealing. He, too, had much to lose by Forrest Bulow's anger. Bulow had apparently found in him qualities that were lacking in his own son, and had built his career. If Helen Quarles had revealed his connection with the murder, how would Claire have reacted? Would she have defended her husband or would she have thrown him to the wolves?

Which brought him to Claire herself. He could easily imagine Claire telling Evelyn that Sylvia was involved in a love affair with Ed Morison. Why had she maintained a correspondence for twenty years with a woman a generation older than herself, not a woman, Mr. Potter would have thought, to build a lasting relationship with a child. Who else could so easily have roused Miss Quarles's fear of Lenny? Who else would Miss Quarles so readily have agreed to meet, alone and at night?

Mr. Potter shook his head. All that he was sure of about Claire was that, long before Paula had been doped, Claire had deliberately dragged out the story of Derek Savage's strange death.

The living room windows of the little Cape Cod cottage were wide open to catch the breeze. Now and then a June bug, with its bass growl, hurled itself against the screen. The fireflies were brighter than Mr. Potter had ever seen them, their lights visible even in the moon-flooded night. He got up to stand at the window, hearing the rustle of maple leaves, seeing the shadows of the little picket fence etched neatly on the lawn, and the dark mass of a rhododendron bush. As he watched, the heavy shadow divided, became two shadows. The head and shoulders of a man were clearly visible. He stood quite still, seeming to watch the house.

Mr. Potter was so intent on the motionless observer that he leaped when a hand touched his shoulder.

"Potter," Kurt said almost soundlessly, "we've got an intruder."

"I know. I've been watching him."

Kurt peered out to look at the silent man beside the rhododendron bush. "Hell, we've got an invasion," he whispered. "There's another one. I just checked to see if Molly was all right and looked out of her window. There's a guy working on the kitchen door."

He pulled out a pencil flashlight and Mr. Potter caught his wrist. "No lights."

He took a last look at the unmoving man in front and started toward the kitchen, with Kurt at his heels.

"He must have come around from the front," he said. "Get the dining room window open, Kurt, if you can handle the screen without making too much noise. You can cut him off if he gets away from me."

Mr. Potter went quietly through the dining room, leaving Kurt to fumble with the window. Cautiously, inch by inch, he eased open the swinging door into the kitchen. He pushed his way through and eased the door shut.

The back door stood wide open and someone was in the kitchen with him. There was a faint sound as clothing brushed against a chair. Then a flashlight beam found the refrigerator. The door was opened and a rapid search was made of the interior, the shelves, the ice trays, the dehydrator, the deep-freeze compartment. Then the door was closed and the same careful search was made of the gas range, the ovens, the trays under the burners.

The searcher was on his knees now, looking under the refrigerator. There was a soft grunt as he lost his balance, and the light went up in a sudden arc, moved, struck Mr. Potter's face. A gasp. The light was switched out and Mr. Potter leaped forward, hurling himself in a low tackle at the intruder's knees, but he had already flung himself toward the door. The screen banged and, as Mr. Potter picked himself up, crooning a soft litany of frustration, he heard feet pounding around the house. There was a muffled grunt as the housebreaker collided with Kurt. A blow was followed by a heavy fall.

By the time Mr. Potter had extricated himself from the kitchen chair with which he had become entangled and had raced back through the house to the front door, the intruder had run down the path to the picket fence and vaulted over it without stopping.

Kurt, in his determination to protect Molly, had put the chain on the door and by the time Mr. Potter had opened it, there was only a shadow on the road. It moved and Mr. Potter recognized the shape and carriage of Ross Bentwick's head. Then it was gone and a motor turned over.

Lights flared on in the living room, half blinding Mr. Potter, and Molly ran down the stairs in blue cotton pajamas and a terry cloth robe, looking about sixteen, her eyes wide with alarm.

"What's happening? Where's Kurt?" She saw his expression. "Hiram, if you've let anything happen to Kurt—"

"Stay here," he told her, and ran out on the porch.

Molly followed him, of course. Under the open dining room window Mr. Potter called softly, "Kurt?" and stumbled, almost falling headlong over the man who lay huddled on the ground. Before he could regain his balance, Molly had pushed him aside and was kneeling, her hands searching the face and head of the unconscious man with frantic haste.

"Kurt? Kurt? Hiram, it's Kurt! He's dead!"

Mr. Potter knelt beside her. "He's not dead," he told her. "He's just knocked out. Can you help me lift him?"

Together they carried him, staggering under his weight, into the living room where they laid him gently on the floor. There was a lump on the side of his head.

"I'll have to leave you while I get a doctor," Mr. Potter said reluctantly. "I'm sorry as hell about this, Molly." He reached into his pocket and pulled out a small revolver. "Do you know how to use this?"

"Kurt and I did some target practice last summer." She took the revolver in a small competent hand. "Don't worry, Hiram," she said grimly. "If anyone comes back tonight, I'll shoot. I'm in this now on my own account."

Twelve

"Knowing you," Molly said bitterly, "is like giving house room to a black widow spider; it's like having a barracuda for a pet; it's like living in the path of a hurricane and watching the barometer fall; it's—"

Captain Foote grinned at his crestfallen friend. "At least, he stirs things up."

Mr. Potter groaned aloud and Molly relented. She poured more coffee for the two men and for Paula Savage, who was curled up on the love seat, wearing a tailored robe. This morning, the shadows under her eyes were as dark as bruises and her skin had a gray pallor. The doctor's treatment, while effective, had been an exhausting business.

"Fortunately," Molly went on more cheerfully, "Kurt has a thick skull. The doctor says he'll be all right. Unless the x-rays show something wrong, the hospital will send him home tomorrow. He has a terrific headache and he can't focus too well and he's nauseated, but there is nothing serious to worry about. Just a mild concussion."

Captain Foote chuckled and Molly gave Mr. Potter a friendly grin.

"Actually, Hiram, he's as proud as punch for tangling with a murderer in defense of his little woman. Watch him or, after a few more tellings, he'll be making it sound like the battle of the century. I can see it coming on. By this morning he had added a bestial growling sound to his assailant. Don't worry about Kurt any more. What I want to know is—what happens next?"

"What I want to know," Paula said, "is what has happened already?"

When Mr. Potter had told her, she pulled the robe

more tightly around her. Her eyes seemed enormous in her white face.

"Drugged! But how was it done?"

"Sleeping pills dissolved in your drink," Mr. Potter explained. "What was in your glass, a Cuba libre?"

She nodded. "I don't like them, but I'd started with daiquiris and thought I'd better stick to rum. So he tried to kill me again; this time right under your nose."

Mr. Potter winced at the unspoken accusation. "This wasn't an attempt to kill you," he said, partly in explanation, partly in exoneration. "There wasn't enough of the stuff. It was intended to make you appear drunk and discredit you so Mr. Morison would chase you out of Coxbury."

"How long," she inquired gently, "do you plan to let Lenny Horgan continue to make these attempts on me, Mr. Potter?"

"Frankly," he admitted, "I have no idea who drugged you last night."

Captain Foote looked at him in surprise. "But I understood that Horgan—"

"What could I believe, in the first place, except that Lenny Horgan was the man I was looking for? I realize we can't eliminate anyone at this point, but from the beginning I've had a kind of idea, a glimmering of a theory. That comment Miss Quarles made—that she wondered who had put Lenny up to killing Evelyn, that she wasn't sure, not sure enough—it suggested someone working behind the scenes. Miss Quarles's anguish at having to testify against Lenny bothered me."

"Just what," Captain Foote demanded, "are you getting at? What do you believe, anyhow?"

"I believe that someone primed Evelyn with the information with which she tried to blackmail Lenny Horgan; I believe Miss Quarles guessed who it was; I believe the guilty person knows that and killed her to keep her still. He's trying to get rid of Mrs. Savage because he thinks Miss Quarles passed on the information to her."

One of Paula's eloquent hands made a slight gesture, instantly checked, as he said Mrs. Savage.

"I'll say this for Mr. Potter," Captain Foote commented. "He can take a nice straightforward situation and mess it up more than anyone I know."

"This never was a straightforward situation," Mr. Potter retorted. He sketched briefly Evelyn Dwight's blackmailing activities.

"Well, I'll be damned," the officer said. "I was looking through some old records just a couple of months ago and found the files on that car-stealing gang. They made a real killing around here twenty years ago. No one ever suspected those kids were involved. What did you find out about this guy?"

"The boys called him Mossback, which Lenny thought was a nickname, and he was tall and thin. Lenny doesn't remember which of them was the original contact."

"I'll see if we can trace him. He may have been operating all over the place."

Mr. Potter turned to Paula. "Has anyone shown any interest in what Miss Quarles said to you?"

"All of them," Paula said dryly. Her face stiffened.

"What is it?" Mr. Potter asked.

To his surprise she flushed vividly. "Ross Bentwick is the only one who knew I would be here last night. And he was angry—that is, he thought I came here as a reporter to get information about Lenny; and then Mr. Tooling overheard a part of a conversation I had with Mr. Morison and misinterpreted it. He was furious because he thought I was trying to undermine Ross by telling his uncle he was a drunk. All four men are incredibly loyal to each other."

She was silent for a moment. "Do you believe," she asked abruptly, "that murder is the worst crime there is?"

"Well, no," Mr. Potter said slowly, "I'm not sure I do. It has always seemed to me that dope-peddling was worse. And starting a war—mass murder. And—"

She nodded. "Ross Bentwick told me, when I spoke of

Lenny being a murderer, that the worst crimes were with-in the law."

"Do you have any idea why a man with his ability has become a drunk?" Mr. Potter asked.

Paula shook her head. Then she nodded it slowly and repeated Ross's comment about gathering Dutch courage to see what twenty years in prison had done to Lenny.

"That sounds to me like a feeling of guilt," Captain Foote said.

"Of course," Paula said, "Stan Tooling might have doped my drink so I'd seem to be drunk, as a kind of re-taliation for hurting Ross with his uncle. You know that's an odd thing. Ross and his uncle are devoted to each oth-er, really, but there's no trust between them. Something went wrong there."

"Let's try to get down to facts, if there are any," Cap-tain Foote said impatiently. "I know that murders have been committed for twenty-five cents or because a father refused to let his kid skip school to go to a baseball game. But these people—it would take a lot of pressure, a whale of a motive, to make any of them kill. When you stop to think of it—"

"I've spent most of the night thinking of it," Mr. Pot-ter told him. "All I have come up with is a lot of ques-tions."

"Let's have some," Foote suggested.

"We know why Lenny killed," Mr. Potter said. "He believed that his stepfather was capable of killing his mother. Personally, I think he was wrong. Forrest Bulow was a bully and he was inordinately possessive, but Len-ny's point of view was warped because the old man frightened him. For all we know, Evelyn's hold over the other boys may have been as baseless as that. They were only sixteen, after all. Apparently, they had one basic fear in common, that if Evelyn told what she knew about them they would be disinherited: Willis by his father, Ross by his uncle. Perhaps I shouldn't use the word dis-inherit in regard to Stan. But certainly he would have been finished with Bulow who was all set to help the boy build a brilliant career. Which he has since done."

"You've forgotten Claire," Paula said.

"It wasn't a woman who knocked Kurt down," Molly said firmly. "No woman could do it, unless maybe," she added, "one of those Soviet women weight-throwers."

"But Claire is wildly jealous of Stan," Paula said. "Anyone could tell. And he was having an affair with Evelyn."

"We don't know anything more about that first crime," Mr. Potter said. "But when we come to the second, to the murder of a defenseless and frightened old woman whose neck was broken, not in a moment of rage or of blind impulse but by deliberate planning, no longer by a sixteen-year-old boy but by a mature person, we have a totally different situation.

"We have to consider that the position has changed. Willis Bulow no longer fears for his inheritance—he's got it; he also has a blindly devoted, almost infatuated, wife, who will stand by him through anything. Where's his motive? Damned if I know.

"Stan is safe, too. Claire has her inheritance and he is in the clear—unless he was behind that first murder. If that's the case, and the fact were to be proved, Claire is not the kind of woman to stand by. He could still lose everything he has achieved.

"When we come to Ross we find a more potent motive. Morison is still alive and he can change his will at any time. Ross seems to be the only one who made no effort to get Lenny freed. And Ross was here last night."

"Ross already knows that his uncle is going to change his will," Paula said. "I was there when Mr. Morison told him so. He is giving half of his money to Lenny because Bulow left him nothing."

"Is he now!" Captain Foote said in a tone of satisfaction. "That must have burned Bentwick."

"It upset him," Paula said, "but I honestly don't think it was the money. I think it was because his uncle had—oh, lost faith in him."

The State Police officer grinned. "I've always understood that Bentwick wows the women."

Paula flushed. "It's not a question of Mr. Bentwick's charm," she said tartly. "It's a question of common justice."

"People around here don't speak so well of him."

"Because he and his uncle don't get along and Mr. Morison is supposed to be infallible or something."

There was a look of surprised speculation in Mr. Potter's face. "None the less," he said quietly, "it occurs to me that the police might keep an eye on Lenny from now on."

"You think he's in danger?" Captain Foote asked.

"I think, in spite of Mrs. Savage's sponsorship, that Bentwick might not shed any tears if Lenny were eliminated from the picture."

"No," Paula said. "I don't believe a word of it."

"Bentwick was here last night," Captain Foote pointed out.

"There were two men," Mr. Potter reminded him, "but I certainly did not get the impression that they were working together. Separate enterprises, in my opinion. The only trouble is that I didn't identify Ross until the very end. I don't know whether he was the housebreaker or—or what," he finished lamely.

Paula shivered. "I begin to feel as though I had got into a haunted house."

"There's one thing for your consolation," Mr. Potter said; "the searching of the house had nothing to do with you. It has gone on summer after summer, at the time when these people are all here."

"But if only one man was searching the cottage, what was the other one doing?" Paula demanded.

"I don't know," Mr. Potter admitted. He added rather fretfully, "I'm not omniscient. But it does occur to me that Ross might possibly have come on your account; he might have worried over your condition, wanted to know whether you were all right, and then stayed on to see what the hell was happening."

"I hope he had a shock when that ambulance drove

up to take Kurt to the hospital," Molly said. "I just hope he did."

"He prob—" Mr. Potter's words were checked by a kingsize yawn.

"Hiram," Molly said, "you ought to be in bed. You haven't had any sleep at all."

"Not yet," he said more briskly. "While Captain Foote is here I want to search this cottage from the roof to the basement. If there's anything here, we are going to find it."

"You're a lawless fellow," Foote remarked. "Without a search warrant—"

"Mr. Morison turned the house over to me," Paula reminded him. "While I'm in residence I have a right to look around if I want to. I heard a mouse. You can be looking for that, if anyone questions you."

Three hours later, Captain Foote dried his hands on a towel. "If there is anything bigger than a postage stamp hidden in this cottage, you can have my next month's salary."

"Of course," Mr. Potter pointed out, "it would help if we knew what we were looking for." He stretched wearily and looked at his watch. "Time for lunch. Let's get some food. But first—what are we going to do with Mrs. Savage? Obviously she can't stay here alone another night."

"She can come to the barn," Molly said. "It will be company for me until Kurt comes home. She can have your room and you can stay here at the cottage."

"I've got to go to New York," Mr. Potter said. "This case is wide open now. I want to know what all these people were doing the night Miss Quarles was killed and the following morning when someone tried to push Mrs. Savage in front of a taxi."

A car motor raced and they watched, fascinated, while Sylvia Bulow maneuvered her cumbersome body from under the wheel and got out of the car. She saw them at the window and waved.

Mr. Potter admitted her and Sylvia said, "I stopped at

Ed's and he told me Mrs. Savage was here. I wanted to know how—" She paused, trying to frame her question tactfully.

Mr. Potter cut in smoothly. "Mrs. Bulow, I don't believe you know Mrs. Jepson. And Captain Foote of the Connecticut State Police. Mrs. Jepson very kindly spent the night here, looking after Mrs. Savage. As you probably guessed, she was drugged last night."

"Drugged." Sylvia spoke heavily. "Drugged." She held out her hands to Paula in mute apology. "My dear, what can I say to you? I am so bitterly sorry, so ashamed. How did it happen?"

"Sleeping pills in her drink," Mr. Potter explained.

Sylvia's heavy face looked dazed. "But that's impossible. The only one who takes sleeping pills is Ivy. And Ivy wouldn't—"

"No," Mr. Potter agreed. "Ivy wouldn't. But I don't suppose she kept them locked up."

"No, any of us could get at them easily. Any of us." Sylvia looked pleadingly at Paula. "What can I do, my dear? What can any of us do to compensate—"

"Captain Foote," Mr. Potter explained, "has come because we've been having some excitement here. Last night, we had two intruders; one of them knocked out Mrs. Jepson's husband who is now in the hospital with a concussion."

"It's as though something had been let loose on us," Sylvia cried.

"Are you regretting—" Mr. Potter began.

"No!" she said. "Find out why all this is happening. We've got to stop it, no matter who gets hurt."

"Where was everyone last night?" he asked.

Sylvia shook her head. She didn't know. She had gone to bed and slept like a log. She would still be asleep, she confessed, if Ross had not awakened her practically at dawn when he came to take Lenny fishing.

She was unaware of the quickened attention of the four people.

"It will be good for Lenny," she said cheerfully. "And Ross is going to show him how to drive that sports car of his."

Mr. Potter shook off his fatigue. "Where were they going, Mrs. Bulow?"

"I have no idea." As she saw his expression the color faded out of her face.

Captain Foote went out to his car, half running, and spoke on the two-way radio. As he came back into the house, his face warned them before he spoke.

"Bentwick's car has been smashed up on Route 25 and the driver has been taken to the New Milford hospital."

"Which—" Sylvia began.

"Lenny Horgan."

"Have him kept under guard," Mr. Potter said. "Don't let anyone get at him. Anyone at all. Where is Bentwick?"

"He was not hurt at all, apparently," Captain Foote said. "A passing car picked him up and took him back to Morison's." He glanced at Sylvia. "You must have just missed him." He turned toward the door. "We won't miss him again."

Thirteen

He would start at the beginning, Mr. Potter decided, and check as he went. From the Gramercy Park house he telephoned O'Toole, his long-suffering detective friend on the homicide squad. He was greeted by a prolonged groan. The newscast, linking Helen Quarles's death with the release of Lenny Horgan, had stirred up the animals.

They had made a routine check. Lenny Horgan had been given permission to spend the night of the Quarles murder in New York with his mother. The apartment she had borrowed had no doorman and no elevator. The neighbors were sure that there had been no party to celebrate his release. It had been a hot night and the people across the hall had left their door propped open. They had seen a heavy-set woman, obviously Mrs. Bulow, let herself into the apartment. She had been alone. They had noticed her because she was a stranger to them and they were acquainted with the regular tenant. By the time they had gone to bed, shortly after eleven o'clock, no one else had entered the apartment.

O'Toole went on gloomily with his report. Of course, that didn't mean that Horgan might not have a cast-iron alibi. He might have been out celebrating with friends.

He hadn't been, Mr. Potter told him. He had spent the evening alone, strolling around New York. And he had walked home through Central Park.

"Where did you get that?" the detective demanded.

"He told me so."

"Maybe, some day," the detective commented after a pause, "you'll break down and tell me how you do it."

"It's my trustworthy face," Mr. Potter assured him. "Anyhow, the case has opened out since I reached Coxbury." Rapidly, but succinctly, he outlined his theory.

"That's fine. That's just fine," O'Toole said. "Now we've got a whole bunch of suspects. And not one single scrap of evidence. What do you—"

"I want to eliminate a few of them, if I can," Mr. Potter explained mildly. "They are bound to have some sort of alibi either for the night of Miss Quarles's murder or the following morning when someone tried to push Mrs. Savage in front of a taxi. Anyone with an alibi for either time should be in the clear."

When he had explained what he wanted to do, the detective warned him, "You are strictly on your own, you understand."

He added, "If you land in jail, don't expect any help from me. I'll come leer at you through the bars."

Mr. Potter took a taxi to the building where Paula Savage had lived. The driver inched his way along the street, sounding his horn to scatter the children who were playing ball, darting around oncoming cars and escaping injury by inches.

The outside door, as Paula had told him, stood wide open. Mr. Potter looked at the row of mailboxes, and rang the bell. A slatternly woman in bedroom slippers opened the door at the rear of the hall.

"Whatcha want?"

"Have you any vacancies?"

She sighed and went back for keys. Mr. Potter followed her up the worn stairs. At the top she stopped to catch her breath.

"Let me," he said politely, and pushed against the door.

"It's locked," she told him.

The door opened against his weight and he stepped back to let her pass him. So far, Paula's story checked. Anyone could have entered her apartment unobserved and, under cover of the electric storm, unheard.

With the windows closed, the apartment was swelteringly hot. It was dark, shabby and inconvenient. Recalling Paula's vivid attractions and Graham Collinge's tribute to her ability as an actress, Mr. Potter was appalled at the conditions under which she had chosen to live rather than lift the veil that hung over her husband's death and endure the harsh spotlight of a return to the stage.

"It's a nice little apartment," the woman told him eagerly. "The young lady who had it only left because she got a job out of town."

Mr. Potter said that he knew the young lady, which was how he had learned of the vacancy.

"By the way," he said vaguely, "there was something she wanted me to—oh, of course, she told me she had turned over to you a bunch of keys on a key ring. I wonder if you still have them."

"There now," the woman said with a short laugh, "I might have known! She gave me a song and dance about someone breaking in and leaving those keys in the lock! And it turns out they were her own keys!" She shook her head, chuckling. "People are the limit!"

"Do you have the keys?"

"They're downstairs, if you want to come along."

In a filthy and cluttered room she searched aimlessly through untidy dresser drawers. It was Mr. Potter who spied the key ring hanging on a nail on the wall. The woman laughed again. Well, now, wasn't he the smart one! And to think the young lady had wanted her to report to the police. She put the keys in Mr. Potter's hand.

He promised vaguely to let her know his decision and left the building. He hadn't really doubted Paula's story but he was glad to have it corroborated.

The employees at the Fifth Avenue building where the Willis Bulows lived were very different from Paula's slatternly superintendent. At sight of the uniformed doorman who hastened to the taxicab, Mr. Potter realized that he should have made some plan in advance instead of trying to play it by ear.

"Good afternoon, Mr. Potter," the doorman said. "It's a long time since you've been here. Not since your mother's death, if I remember correctly."

Mr. Potter took a quick glance at the building and tried to remember why it was so familiar. One of his mother's friends, apparently, had lived there at one time, but who—he prodded his memory. He had a vague impression of rooms cluttered with Victorian furniture, of tea served in paper-thin cups, of conversations devoted to genealogy. Who could they have been?

The attendant pushed back the heavy glass door. "Do you wish to be announced, sir, or are the Wendlesons expecting you?"

The Wendlesons were a tiny couple, who seemed to have shrunk during the intervening years. Twenty minutes later, over tea and toasted muffins, Mr. Potter found himself involved in a discussion about his family tree. In this apartment time had stood still. All that was lacking was the presence of his mother, with her booming voice.

After a proper interval, Mr. Potter steered the conversation from the changes he had made in the Gramercy Park house since his mother's death, to the Fifth Avenue building, and then, by easy stages, to the Willis Bulows, tenants in the building whose acquaintance he had recently made.

"Hiram," Mrs. Wendleson said severely, but with an unexpected twinkle in her faded eyes, "don't be so ridiculous. Heaven knows, it has taken you long enough to come to the point. Stop beating around the bush and tell me what you want to know about the Bulows. I suppose you've got yourself mixed up in that unsavory Horgan murder case."

He grinned ruefully and, sure of their discretion, explained that he wanted, if possible, to find out where Willis Bulow had been Thursday night and Friday morning.

"I suppose we mustn't ask why you want to know," the old lady told him in a tone of resignation, "but Walter can find out for you. We've lived here for nearly thirty years. As a matter of fact, Walter owns the building, though we never tell people so for fear they'll come to us with their complaints. Anyhow, he can learn what the building employees know."

She nodded her white head at her husband. "Go on, Walter," she said firmly.

With an amused look from one to the other, her husband obediently went to the telephone. By the time Mr. Potter had docilely drunk another cup of tea—how much tannin he had absorbed during his dutiful years as his mother's escort!—Mr. Wendleson had gathered all the information that he could.

"I don't know what you have in mind in regard to young Bulow," he said, "but you aren't going to be able to establish an alibi for him here. I called the manager who questioned the elevator men and the hallmen. All the Bulow servants had Thursday night off to attend the wedding of the butler's daughter. There's no record of any guests being announced during the evening. The man on the elevator was new and there was a big party that night. So many strange faces that he has no idea who came in and went out."

Wendleson made the lighting of a cigar an elaborate ritual and Mr. Potter grinned at him. "He only does it to annoy because he knows it teases," he told his hostess, who said, "Walter, don't be childish! What did you find out?"

Wendleson chuckled. "The doorman saw nothing of Mrs. Bulow from the time when she came home late in the afternoon. He is certain she did not go out again because she would either have used her own car or called a taxi, and in either case he would have known of it. But he saw Bulow twice: once when he came home in the early evening and a second time when he returned around midnight. He was walking and he had been drenched by the rain. That's why the doorman remembered. He doesn't know when Bulow went out. All he is sure of is that he was rushed off his feet just before theater time getting cabs for five different tenants. Mr. Bulow could easily have left the building at that time without being observed."

"And Friday morning?"

"The Bulows left separately and did not return until about eleven when they sent for their car and drove to the country."

With a glance at his watch Mr. Potter got up to take

his leave, thanking his host for his trouble.

"What I want to know," Mrs. Wendleson said, "is does it help?"

"It just raises more questions," Mr. Potter admitted.

She put a tiny clawlike hand on his arm. "When it's all over, will you come back and tell us?"

When he had given his promise, he walked the few blocks to the smart little town house on the East Side where the Toolings lived. For a few moments he stood looking at the house while he finished a cigarette. The easygoing Stan Tooling had flourished mightily with the help and guidance of the irascible Forrest Bulow.

He hesitated for a moment and then, tossing away the cigarette, he ran briskly up the three neat steps and made the knocker resound. The door was opened by a trim housemaid wearing an organdie cap and an apron with huge bows. She looked, Mr. Potter thought, more like a soubrette in a musical comedy than like the type of house servant who was available in the contemporary world.

In response to his anxious question, she shook her head. The Toolings were not at home; they had gone away for the summer. Mr. Potter looked helpless in his consternation. He had just flown in from England that morning and he had been desperately eager to see Mr. Tooling. Perhaps, if he could write a note, she would give him Mr. Tooling's summer address.

There were times when Mr. Potter was reconciled to his utterly respectable appearance. The maid looked at his guileless face and invited him in.

"There's a desk in Mr. Tooling's study," she said, "and paper and ink. You can write to him there."

When she had supplied him with writing materials and the Coxbury address, the maid hovered uncertainly.

He picked up the pen and frowned at the paper. "Let's see," he said in a worried tone, "just when did I try to call him from London? Thursday, wasn't it? Thursday evening. Now with the difference in time, that would have been—"

"Thursday evening, sir?" the maid said helpfully.

"That's the night before they went away." She thought for a moment. "Madam had the telephone shut off almost all day Thursday because the reporters kept calling. About that," her voice dropped, "that convict who is related to Madam and who got out of prison. An awful thing, to be sure. I was glad when she said she wouldn't want us in the evening. I wasn't looking forward to opening the door to any jail bird, I can tell you."

"Dear me," Mr. Potter ejaculated. "I should think not. But surely Mrs. Tooling wouldn't take such a chance herself?"

The girl shrugged her shoulders. "The three of us, the cook, the houseman and me, played gin rummy all evening upstairs. I'm sure I don't know whether anyone came or not. Mr. Tooling left this room so cluttered that I guess he worked here the whole time. Madam went out in the late afternoon and in the evening—though she said she went to bed with a bad headache—"

"Said?" Mr. Potter repeated the word with flattering attention.

"I know Madam's headaches," the girl said. "Whenever he don't jump through a hoop fast enough to suit her she goes to her room with a bad headache. But she don't often stay there."

"Difficult to work for, is she?" Mr. Potter asked sympathetically.

"Well, everything's got to be just so and no excuses. I'd as soon shoot a policeman as break a bit of glassware in this house. And snoopy. Trying to listen to his telephone calls and going through his desk when he isn't home. But not such a bad place, on the whole. The pay is good and he is as nice a man as you'd want to work for. Anything goes with him. No complaints when something comes unstuck and always a thank you when you do something for him."

"Oh, how stupid of me," Mr. Potter exclaimed. "It wasn't Thursday when I telephoned from London; it was Friday morning."

The maid shook her head. "The telephone was working then and I answered it myself. Madam went out early to get a new bathing suit and he was to pick up the car and meet her at Abercrombie's. Then they went on to the country. There was no call from England or anywheres abroad, I'm sure of that."

Mr. Potter nodded thoughtfully, scribbled a few lines, sealed the envelope and put down the pen.

"Thank you very much," he said. "I'll get this in the mail at once for Mr. Tooling."

Two blanks, he thought, when he was out on the hot street again. All I need now is to find that Ross Bentwick has no alibi and the wheel will have come full circle.

There were a few people sitting on benches in Washington Square as his taxi turned west and a few sightseers strolling along the streets, looking for signs of the Village which has largely vanished with the years, and half expecting to see Edna St. Vincent Millay turn the next corner, her bright hair blowing in the wind.

Ross Bentwick's superintendent answered his ring promptly. He was an Irishman in his late thirties, intelligent and cleanly, with an ingratiating smile.

"Yes, sir?"

"A friend of mine suggested I talk to you about an apartment. He wasn't sure whether you have a vacancy but he is so comfortable himself—"

"One of our present tenants, sir?"

"Yes; that is, I haven't seen him recently; he may have moved. Mr. Ross Bentwick."

"Oh, Mr. Bentwick. Sorry, we haven't a vacancy right now. There will be two in the fall, but—what size would you be wanting?"

"Bentwick's setup sounded ideal for my purposes."

"We'll have a nice terrace apartment with five rooms and a small one like Mr. Bentwick's; not a garden apartment, of course; this will be on the second floor, but the layout is the same."

"I suppose I couldn't see it."

"Not very well, sir. The lady is at home. But—" He hesitated, sized up Mr. Potter. "As you are a friend of

Mr. Bentwick's, I don't know why you can't look at his."

When he had unlocked the door, he gave a little exclamation of distress. The room was cluttered with glasses and dirty clothing; a newspaper had fallen in the middle of the floor.

"It's really a nice apartment but Mr. Bentwick got a telegram; he had to leave in a hurry. That's why the place hasn't been cleaned up. He's—" The superintendent looked from the telltale glasses to Mr. Potter.

"Well," he said rather defiantly, "if you know him you can see as good as I can that he sometimes gets a drop too much. But I'll tell you straight, and it's God's truth, I'd rather deal with Mr. Bentwick drunk than most people sober. He has a quick temper and he hits the bottle, but he's an all-right guy. If I got in trouble I'd sooner go to him than to anyone I can think of, and that includes my own family. He might give me hell for making a fool of myself but he would try to do something about it."

Mr. Potter smiled. "I don't know a nicer recommendation." He looked around the apartment, noticed that the newspaper bore headlines about Lenny Horgan's release from prison. "I'll let you know my decision about the apartment. Sorry I missed Mr. Bentwick. I called him a couple of times this week, Thursday evening and Friday morning—"

The Irishman shook his head. "He must have been barcrawling Thursday. I heard him come in, nearly morning, and, brother, was he loaded! I thought he'd sleep it off half the next day but he was up bright and early; came to tell me he'd had a telegram calling him away and he had to buy himself some new shirts. He'd forgot to send his dirty ones to the laundry. Then he was going to get his car—have you seen it?" He whistled appreciatively. "He came back with the car and got his suitcase and that's the last I saw of him."

Not an alibi in a carload, Mr. Potter thought in discouragement, as he came out onto the street. And yet each of these people might be able to produce half a dozen witnesses as to where and how they had spent the critical times. To find the witnesses, however, there would have to be publicity, which was to be avoided if possible.

Mr. Potter looked at his watch. Nearly six. What he needed at this point was a long cold drink. No, he told himself virtuously. Work first, pleasure afterwards. He looked around for a telephone booth, considered that Graham Collinge might not be eager to see him, and decided to call on him without advance notice.

When he sent his name up from the lobby of the building on Central Park South he saw, by the operator's expression, that Collinge had made an uncomplimentary remark.

"You may go up, sir," he said with some reserve. "The penthouse. Elevator on your left."

There were half a dozen people in the big living room, drinking, talking and laughing above the determined sound of jazz being beaten out on the piano by a famous violinist. Mr. Potter recognized a popular actress, a man who was as well-known for being an *enfant terrible* as for his abstract paintings, the controversial M.C. of a successful television program, a dress designer whose name was a household word and whose own clothes were incredibly dowdy, and a Broadway columnist.

Collinge came forward to greet him. "Hail, bird of ill omen."

As the columnist darted toward him, Mr. Potter said, "Is there any place where we can talk for a few minutes? Just ten minutes." He turned to the columnist who had grasped his arm. "Scram," he said firmly.

"Have a heart, Potter. What's all this about Lenny Horgan?"

"Horgan?" Mr. Potter said in wide-eyed surprise. "I have no idea."

The columnist snorted. "I checked your house yesterday to see what you were up to. You're usually good for a story. I found you'd gone to Coxbury. Why Coxbury, I asked myself."

"And what did you answer yourself?" Mr. Potter said politely.

"Echo answered 'Horgan.' Are you looking into the Quarles woman's death? Have you seen Horgan? What—"

Answering his mute appeal, Collinge ruthlessly detached the columnist and took Mr. Potter into a small, austerely furnished workroom, with a battered desk, a utilitarian table, a straight chair, a typewriter, a set of plain green office files, and a fine light.

He paused at the door to order a drink for Mr. Potter, satisfyingly long and cold, and then offered his uninvited guest the desk chair and wedged his hip against the side of the table.

"What is it this time?"

Mr. Potter sighed. "By some hard fate," he lamented, "I'm about as welcome as the bubonic plague."

"I can't imagine why," Collinge said unsympathetically. He went to the door to get Mr. Potter's drink. "I searched the morning papers for indications of mayhem, earthquake and mass murder in Coxbury, but all seems quiet on the northern front. Paula okay?"

"Aside," Mr. Potter told him, "from the fact that someone doped a drink for her last night, she's doing as well as could be expected. Actually, quite a lot has been happening."

"I couldn't be less surprised."

When Mr. Potter had finished his story, Collinge whistled soundlessly. "It's one hell of a mess. But if you've come to me for alibis, I can't help you. I never heard of the Bulows and Toolings until you brought these unsavory characters into my life. The only one of the lot I know is Bentwick and I certainly didn't see him Thursday night or Friday morning. Matter of fact, I haven't seen or heard of him in months. Not since he dropped out of *The Poisoner*. What are you running up there: a port of missing actors?"

"Why did Bentwick leave *The Poisoner*?"

"He began hitting the bottle; for a while he pulled himself together for performances, and then he just didn't seem to give a damn. He fell apart. Even then, I think they'd have kept him on, hoping for the best, but he walked out one Saturday night and that was that."

"Why?"

Collinge didn't know. Bentwick was tops as an actor; he'd never been cast in sympathetic parts but he was able to handle anything: tragedy, comedy, romantic plays, farce, even—Collinge grinned deprecatingly—his own symbolic plays.

"Do you like him?" Mr. Potter asked.

"I've never been close to him, but I think it would be hard not to like him; he's wonderful company, with an infectious sense of humor. Not given to stealing the limelight, just a hell of a good fellow."

"Cheerful type, I gather."

Collinge gave Mr. Potter a shrewd look. "Okay, Machiavelli, not a cheerful type. Not recently. The sanguine types don't become chronic drunks, as I don't need to tell you. But don't ask me why because I don't know. Closest I ever came to it was one Saturday night after the show; a bunch of us were hanging around that Third Avenue saloon—you know the place?—and he was getting oiled. By the way, this is a recent thing, you know. Anyhow, I tried to hold him off the fourth drink and Bentwick said, 'It's easier to take when you're out cold.' I said, 'What is?' and he said, 'Being a chivalrous heel.' Queer way to put it, wasn't it? I said, 'Kick the wench out,' and he laughed and said she wasn't his wench, thank God. And I said something about why not forget her and he said—this is what I'm leading up to—'Conscience doth make cowards of us all.' "

"And that's all?"

"That's all," Collinge said firmly. He turned his glass around in his fingers, drained it and set it down. "Ready for a refill?"

Mr. Potter shook his head.

"Come in and join the crowd."

"I wish I could, but I've got to get back to Coxbury. May I call home first, in case—"

At Collinge's nod, he reached for the telephone and dialed his number. The phone rang for a long time. Tito, he supposed, was outside, gossiping with the superintendent from the apartment building next door.

"God, what a pair they'd make," Collinge said suddenly. "Bentwick and Savage. Marvelous in *Much Ado about Nothing*, where they would be perfect foils for each other. Or *Pygmalion*. Or—"

Tito answered breathlessly. He was delighted that Mr. Potter had called. There was a telegram for him. As Mr. Potter stretched out his hand and moved his fingers, Collinge obligingly handed him a paper and pencil. He watched as Mr. Potter wrote down the words.

"Return Coxbury at once. All hell breaking loose. Kurt Jepson."

Fourteen

"I didn't" Molly said, "expect you to sing for your supper. Did you hypnotize them?"

Paula gave her a conspiratorial grin. "I just said, in a lowered voice, 'Isn't it incredible what you can find in these places? When I started to work here yesterday, I couldn't believe my eyes. An original Jepson! I doubt if these people have the slightest idea what they've got. It should never be out here on the road. I do hope they have it insured.' And they took one look and bought it for two hundred dollars and were thrilled to death in the bargain. As they drove off I distinctly heard the woman say, 'An original Jepson! I can't believe it.'"

If that didn't cure Kurt, Molly said, nothing could do it. He had been in more of a rage than she had ever seen him over the destruction of the other canvas.

"I feel guilty about him," Paula said. "If it hadn't been for me, he wouldn't be involved in all this; he'd never have gone to the Quarles cottage and got himself knocked out."

"I have a hunch," Molly said shrewdly, "that's your main trouble. Feeling guilty."

There was something, Paula told her bitterly, about knowing someone wanted her to die, that made her wonder if, perhaps, it was justified.

"That's morbid," Molly said firmly, "and unhealthy. And it is not a bit like you, really. You simply got trapped in something, and you've got to tell yourself you are not to blame. There's enough pain in this world without imaginary suffering and self-punishment. What we've got to do is to figure out the things that are real—to find out who is trying to harm you."

She'd been doing that, Paula said. She kept going over

and over all the people in the Horgan case, wondering which one.

"I look at them," she said, clenching her hands, "and think: 'Did you try to push me in front of that taxi?' "

There was Willis, who, for a fleeting moment in his car, had frightened her. There was Stan who had insisted on her coming to the party where she had been drugged. There was Claire who had brought out publicly the fact of Derek's death, leaving a whole cloud of conjecture behind her, like an octopus in a cloud of its own ink. There was Ross, who had wanted to send her back to New York, who thought she had tried to undermine him with his uncle. Which one? Which one?

She sat staring out onto the highway, remembering that odd scene when Morison had told Ross that he was going to change his will; she recalled the sickness in Ross's face; she felt again the charged horror of the moment when Captain Foote had come back to tell them that Lenny Horgan had been smashed up in Ross Bentwick's car.

Abruptly, she shook her head. "No," she said aloud, "I don't believe it. I simply don't believe it."

Molly took a homemade cigarette out of the little contraption which had rolled it and looked enviously at Paula. "What a lot of things seem to happen to you! Nothing has ever happened to me that was at all exciting except Kurt."

"You are a very lucky girl," Paula told her.

Molly nodded emphatically. "Of course," she admitted judiciously, "Kurt never had a chance. I took one look at him and simply went overboard. But sometimes I wonder —suppose I'd married another man and then met Kurt. How awful! Or suppose I'd never met him at all."

She settled herself cautiously on a rickety chair, after blowing off the dust, and curled up her slender brown legs under her. "You weren't so lucky, were you?"

"No," Paula said. "I wasn't so lucky."

"Do you want to get it out of your system," Molly asked quietly, "or shall we just forget it?"

"I'll never forget it."

"Then," Molly said practically, "you had better talk."

At first, it wasn't easy, but the words, which came with such difficulty in the beginning, began to flow more quickly, and finally tumbled over one another. Paula's parents had died, she said, and she had no immediate family. There had been enough money for her education and after her first year at college she had joined a theatrical group. Derek had been there.

She tried to find words for Derek, for her feeling about him. He was extraordinarily good looking and women pursued him. From the beginning he had fallen for Paula and she was flattered, but she wasn't ready for marriage, and she wasn't really in love with him. They had their work in common and she was fond of him. It was only when she realized how terribly he needed her to provide a kind of stability that she accepted him.

Molly nodded. "One of those," she said.

"What do you mean?"

"A mama's boy, spoiled by women, looking for a mother, mistress, cook, housekeeper, and probably wage-earner, all in one. Those guys who say, 'I need you!' There ought to be a law."

The marriage hadn't worked out, even at the start. Derek was one of those men who can't pass a mirror without stopping to admire themselves. He had an incredible amount of vanity coupled with a growing sense of failure. Even his looks couldn't make him a successful actor, though he would probably have done adequately in movies. But his self-esteem was at stake.

"Wanted to play *Lear*, I suppose."

Paula smiled faintly. "Not *Lear*. He had a profile."

"*Hamlet,* no less!"

"Well, things had started badly and then worsened. There had been women, several women. At the same time, Derek was corroded by jealousy of Paula, though she had never given him the slightest cause. At length, she had decided to leave him.

Her hands clenched hard together. She had started to

leave the apartment and found that Derek had locked the door and pocketed the key. He threatened her. She would never leave him except by the death of one or the other. Then he begged, pleaded, cried—

"It was ghastly," Paula said.

Finally, he had taken a revolver from the desk drawer and flourished it, threatening her, and then turned it on himself. If she left him, he warned her, he would kill himself. And he pulled the trigger. He had forgotten the revolver was loaded. She could see his face now, blankly incredulous—and then no expression at all as he fell at her feet.

After that, she said, there was the inquest, and a woman who had been in love with Derek had called her a murderess. And after that—

"Wait," Molly said, "you're skipping. What went wrong at the inquest? Didn't you tell them how it was?"

"That it was an accident, yes."

"But not what he was like? Not why he did it?"

"But he was dead," Paula said in surprise. "He couldn't defend himself."

Molly reached out to brush Paula's cheek lightly with her fingertips. "You're a fool," she said, "but an awfully nice fool. So then you began to hide."

"Not exactly. I just gave up the stage. I found I couldn't face people and all the talk."

"If you want my opinion," Molly said coolly, "I think it is high time you forgot the guy. You honestly think you are to blame, don't you?"

"I can't forget what Miss Quarles said to me: 'You don't know what it is to live with the fact that you've destroyed a man's life.'"

"Boy, are you in a bad way! There's just one thing for you to do, Paula. Go out and fall in love with another man, head over heels in love with him."

"Just like that," Paula said with a short laugh.

Molly nodded her brown head emphatically. "Just like that. With your looks and charm, you could get any man you wanted. You should hear Kurt; he drools over your beauty. He wants to paint you."

"That," Ross said from the doorway, "is a sound idea. If Jepson paints your portrait I'll buy it. After all, he owes me a picture. I wanted to buy one of his canvases and now they are both gone."

He spoke lightly but his attractively ugly face was anxious as he came into the barn and stood looking down at the two girls.

"How are you?" he asked.

"All right," Paula said.

"Sylvia has just been telling Uncle Ed that you were drugged at Claire's party. We all owe you a most profound apology. We're grovelling, if that's any satisfaction. And I have a note for you from Uncle Ed. You're to come back at once and take my room. I'll move over to the Quarles cottage."

As Paula hesitated to accept the note he held out, he warned her with a grin, "Uncle Ed said if I didn't bring you back, he'd get out of bed and come for you himself. He means it, too."

Something in his voice brought Molly's eyes alertly to his face. She glanced at Paula and then, with her eyebrows raised and a faint smile on her lips, she wandered out of the antique shop and went upstairs.

"Please come," Ross said urgently. "Something is brewing; I don't like it and neither does Uncle Ed. We won't have any peace until you are under our—his—roof."

The man's personality was so strong it seemed to engulf her. She fought against it. She had no intention of being dominated.

"That's quite a change in you," she commented.

"I was afraid you heard me the day you came. But that had nothing to do with you. It was just—you can't help but have seen that there's something wrong between Uncle Ed and me. It's been growing for a long time. Sometimes I think he suspects me of having had some hand in Evelyn's death, of letting Lenny take the rap for me. I'm not sure. He's a hell of a good guy but I can't get through his—distrust—any more. I had a kind of idea if I could help with his book, be around a while, we might patch things up."

His face was stained a dark red. "There's one small point. I don't know whether you got the same idea Sylvia had, but I'd like to assure you that I did not try to kill Lenny this morning in my car in order to prevent him from inheriting half of Uncle Ed's money."

"But I didn't think so," Paula assured him. "Not for a minute."

"The brakes had been tampered with before we set off," Ross explained. "The police have checked the wreckage. I thought I'd better get this clear. You're not, on the whole, a trusting type, are you, my lady Disdain?"

"So far, I haven't had much occasion to be."

Again there was that anxious look on his face. "Sorry. I seem to have done everything I could to make you dislike me." As she started to speak he put his hand over hers in a gesture that was mutely appealing. "And don't say that it doesn't matter. I know—I think we both know —that it does matter. I realize I haven't a chance now. I don't deserve one. But if you've noticed, I'm trying to get the drinking under control. Given a motive, I can perform miracles."

He stopped himself with an exclamation of shocked disgust. "Good God! I'm not asking you to reform me. I'm not asking you to be the reward of my virtuous actions. But when I'm less of a mess I'll come back to this subject." He grinned at her. "Fair warning."

He couldn't be in earnest, of course. They didn't know each other. He wowed women. It was just a habit, a kind of reflex.

"About the drinking," she said awkwardly, "I'd like you to know that Stan Tooling misinterpreted what Mr. Morison was saying to me. I didn't try to make you out a drunk. Your uncle was asking about your acting, whether you were good, why—"

She met his eyes and her own widened in a look of astonishment.

He nodded. "That's the way it is," he told her.

"No," Paula said almost angrily. "This is nonsense. Ridiculous nonsense. Ross Bentwick in his much-publicized rôle as the—what did Captain Foote say?—the man who wows women."

"But that my lady Beatrice should know me and not know me," he quoted soberly. "I am not so reported: it is the base, the bitter disposition of Beatrice that puts the world in her person, and so gives me out. Well, I'll be revenged as I may."

Without warning he drew her into his arms and bent his head so that his mouth met hers. At length he released her.

"So," he said, breathing as though he had been running, "that's the way it is. A clean slate for us both, Paula. We're both guilt-ridden and ghost-ridden; we've been punishing ourselves long enough, don't you agree? And for what, in God's name? We have to start over. Neither of us can do it alone. But together—"

His smile warmed his face. He kissed her again. "I'm rehearsing," he told her, "for my best rôle—Benedick the married man."

"But, Ross—"

"I'm rushing things but I have a curious feeling that everything around us is rushing at runaway speed toward some sort of disaster. There's no time to lose. And that reminds me, poor Uncle Ed is waiting."

She was aware that her hands were not altogether steady as she opened Morison's note, urging her to return to his house at once.

"Please come," Ross said again, watching her face. "He will worry if you don't, and that's not good for him."

"But there's nothing to worry about now." Paula heard the exultant note in her voice that betrayed her but she did not mind. Happiness made her courageous.

"There's something," he said gravely. "I told you something is brewing. The attempt to smash my car is not the only thing that has happened. The villagers are stirred up as hell about Lenny. They are doing their best to make us drive him away. Stan Tooling had his tires slashed to bits during the night. The picture windows at Willis's house have been broken by rocks. The whole hostile attitude is accelerating all the time, like a wheel rolling downhill. And violence engenders violence."

Suddenly he was very close beside her and his hand had covered hers, holding it tightly. "Paula, don't look like that."

"Stop worrying about me! Lenny is the one who is in danger. Suppose they find out where he is. He ought to be moved to some other hospital where he'll be hidden more safely. He ought to be guarded. Call the State Police, Ross, quickly!"

"Ivy's friend Potter has already taken care of that."

"He's my friend, too," Paula said. It was important that he should know she trusted him. She told him about her experiences in New York and explained why she had called on Mr. Potter for help.

When she had finished he was silent for a long time. He was white-faced.

"Ross," she began hesitantly, "why were you outside Miss Quarles's cottage last night? Are you the one who searched it?"

"I was worried about you, and I didn't," he added harshly, "know then how much reason I had to be worried. But Potter was a stranger to me and I didn't like the idea of his taking you home when you weren't—yourself. I came along to make sure that you were all right. Then I saw—I saw someone get into the cottage and later I realized Potter and Jepson were both around and there was trouble. When I saw a woman turn on the light upstairs I knew you were being looked out for."

"Who got into the cottage?"

Ross shook his head. "I don't know what to do; I don't know what in hell to do. I thought I had it figured but—"

He turned to look out at the highway, frowning. "Has it struck you that there are an unusual number of people going by? Something's up."

He took hold of her wrist, holding it so hard that he hurt her. "Something's up!" he said again more sharply.

"There's a mob gathering. I'm going to call the hospital and make sure Lenny is all right."

He ran up the stairs and tapped on the door. Molly pointed to the telephone. When he had made his call, she stopped him before he hung up. "Have them tell Kurt," she said. "If the mob is going to the hospital, Kurt ought to be warned."

Fifteen

By nine o'clock that night when Mr. Potter reached Coxbury even an outsider would have been aware that some unusual ferment was working among the people of the village. They stood in small groups that lacked all the convivial quality of neighborly gatherings. There was no laughter. There were few words. They simply waited in sullen silence.

Mr. Potter was not alone. There was a large, good-looking man with him who, in spite of his well-cut business suit, was obviously either a police official or an army officer. Fierce pressure and what the detective from the New York homicide squad darkly referred to as blackmail had persuaded him to come to Coxbury.

Before they reached the outskirts of the village, O'Toole had pointed out the unusual number of cars on the road.

"Trouble brewing," he said briefly.

"You needn't," Mr. Potter complained, "act as though I were responsible for stirring up a mob."

"Wouldn't put it past you," the other replied.

They drew up before the State Police Barracks where they found Captain Foote. Mr. Potter told him about the telegram he had received from Kurt Jepson.

"Your friend is right," Foote said grimly. "There's hell to pay. The villagers have gone crazy. They are working themselves up to mob frenzy. If they could get their hands on Lenny Horgan right now they would lynch him. They think he's a homicidal maniac and that no one is safe while he is around. We've never had anything like this before. I'd have said it couldn't happen here.

"Right now I have a man patrolling past the old picnic grounds every hour. That's where all outdoor meetings have been held for years. If any people begin to collect there we'll know what we are up against. I've alerted other barracks in case of an emergency."

The mob, he went on to explain, had begun to gather early that morning. What had started it no one knew. A word, a hint, a threat, little things, little deadly things, that turned individual fears and dislike into the collective spirit that is a mindless and irresponsible mob.

"Where is Horgan now?" Mr. Potter asked.

"We smuggled him out of the hospital for fear they would find out where he is and cause trouble for the other patients. He's at Morison's house now. The doctor said he could be moved."

"How badly hurt was he in that car smash?"

"He has some broken ribs and some bad cuts on his face and he lost a few teeth. Uncomfortable as all hell, probably, but when you consider that the car was practically demolished, he's not too bad off. Bentwick wasn't even scratched. One of those freak accidents."

"Was it?" Mr. Potter asked.

Foote nodded. "We were off the beam on that. Bentwick seems to be completely in the clear. The brakes had been tampered with. Unless Bentwick was set on suicide, he'd never have planned an accident that, except for sheer luck, would have killed them both. And it wasn't the only damage that has been done. It's part of a regular reign of terror. Tooling's tires were slashed, the Bulow windows have been stoned. The violence is growing by the hour. You can almost feel it."

"Have you found out anything else?"

"We traced that fellow who headed the car-stealing gang. The one they called Mossback. He's gone up as a fourth offender. One of our men talked to him. It was Willis Bulow he contacted in the first place and Bulow organized the car-stealing gang for this area. Did you pick up anything in New York?"

"Not an alibi for the lot, so far as I could tell. Not until the police can do a real check. The only thing is that Willis was out at the critical time and came home, soaking wet, from walking in the rain."

"There's nothing left but to throw it wide open and give the case publicity," Foote said heavily.

"Later, perhaps," Mr. Potter said. "But there's no time now. We've got hours, minutes perhaps, to stop this mob and we can't do it without more men than you can provide or without clearing Lenny of the Quarles murder."

"That can't be done in minutes," Foote said bluntly.

"It has to be," Mr. Potter told him, his face set, "or an innocent man is going to be killed."

He left the two police officers in consultation and drove to the red barn. As the Volkswagen pulled in, a ghastly apparition staggered down the outside stairs, Kurt Jepson with his head wrapped in enough gauze to make a Turkish turban.

He greeted Mr. Potter with relief. "I got out of the hospital and came home to keep an eye on Molly."

"Where is Mrs. Savage? Isn't she with you?"

"Bentwick came to take her back to the Morison house." Kurt added, "Molly says she is positive that it's all right to let her go."

"Where do the villagers think Horgan is hiding?"

"At the Bulow house."

"Do the Bulows know what is brewing?"

Kurt shrugged. He'd heard the windows had been smashed so they must have a faint idea. Otherwise, he didn't know.

Mr. Potter went upstairs where he found Molly huddled in a chair, her eyes wide with horror.

"Oh, Hiram, I didn't know hate was like this!"

"It's collective madness. Tomorrow they will be ashamed to face themselves."

"But by tomorrow—"

"The State Police are on the job. They won't let the situation get out of control," he told her with what he knew was quite unfounded optimism. There are never enough police.

He dialed the Bulow number and got no response. At length the operator cut in. "That number," she said, "is out of order."

Mr. Potter ran out and got in his car. "I'm going to the Bulow house," he shouted back to Kurt. "Their telephone lines have been cut."

He switched on the motor and started to turn on the lights. Ahead, on the upper level, flames licked out, reaching up into the night. From the lower village came the hoarse hoot of the fire alarm.

Kurt staggered out to the car.

"Get the hell back to the barn," Mr. Potter said. "You are in no condition to go along." As Kurt fumbled with the door, he said brutally, "You'll just be in the way."

He found it difficult to get up the road because of the number of cars and pedestrians that almost blocked it. At first, he assumed that they were hastening to help fight the fire; then, seeing that they were in no hurry to press forward, he thought they were the usual watchers who emerge from nowhere to look at any spectacle. He sounded his horn and almost grazed pedestrians who made no attempt to move aside and let him pass; he inched his way past the parked cars that cluttered the highway.

Then he pulled up on the road before the Bulow house. He saw at a glance that it was too late. The frame structure was already a mass of flames.

He backed his car down the road where there would be no danger of exploding gasoline and ran back. Unrecognizable figures were moving in the darkness, lighted weirdly by the red flickering glow of the fire. What puzzled Mr. Potter was that there were so few fire-fighters. He made them out to be Stan, Willis, Ivy, and the servants from the Bulow and Tooling houses. Sylvia stood far back, watching. Still farther back, a group of villagers, ominously silent, saw without any attempt to check it the destructive work of the fire.

As Mr. Potter hurried forward to help, a woman crossed the lawn at a run and flung up her arms.

"He isn't here," she shouted to the silent villagers, and Mr. Potter recognized her voice. It was Claire Tooling. "Lenny Horgan isn't here."

She wheeled and ran across the lawn toward her own house.

When they realized that she had told them the truth, they began to move quietly away.

As timbers fell with a shower of sparks, Mr. Potter seized Sylvia and drew her, stone-faced, frozen, farther away from the flames. Then he ran forward to get Ivy.

"The whole place is going," he shouted. "There is nothing you can do. You'll only get hurt."

She nodded and called Willis. Only Stan continued to fight the fire like a demon, until Willis pulled him away. Stan came toward the little group, wiping his forehead, which was streaked with black. His shirt stuck damply to his shoulders.

"Where's Claire?" he asked.

"She went home to look after her possessions and make sure the mob couldn't get in," Sylvia said dryly.

"You'd better all come over," he said wearily. "At least the house is stone and the roof is slate. They can't burn that one down." He was staggering as they started across the lawn toward the other house. "When the fire department comes—"

"They won't come, Stan," Ivy said quietly. "They won't come."

Stan motioned the servants to go to his house and turned, putting his arm around Sylvia.

Mr. Potter checked Willis and Ivy as they were about to follow.

"They mean business," he said, looking at the burning house.

"Thank God," Ivy said unexpectedly, "the house is gone. Willis is free, at last, and he can live where he likes and how he likes."

"Can you, Bulow?" Mr. Potter asked quietly.

"Why—I don't see—"

"This isn't just a question of a house burning down, a

house that is probably covered adequately by insurance. It's a question of wanton destruction, of rising mob spirit, of an attempt to burn out Lenny Horgan."

"Lenny is safe," Willis said.

"For how long? There's only one chance for him, and you know it. That is to get the truth about Helen Quarles's murder. Who killed her, Bulow?"

Willis shook his head.

"Where were you the night she was killed?"

"What are you trying to do?" Ivy cried. "Are you claiming that Willis is a murderer?"

"We have some nice evidence," Mr. Potter said, "that seems to point that way."

"Willis couldn't kill anyone. I'm disappointed in you, Mr. Potter. I thought—"

"Wait," he said. "See what you make of these facts:

"a. Willis hated Evelyn because she had humiliated him and caused him extreme emotional disturbance.

"b. He was so afraid that she would make a public laughing stock of him that he agreed to organize a car-stealing gang to raise the money for which she had an insatiable craving.

"c. He knew that if his father discovered his involvement with Evelyn he would be thrown out and disinherited."

"But all that was twenty years ago," Ivy cried. "Because Willis got into trouble as a boy, it doesn't mean he would injure a harmless old woman now."

"Miss Quarles was not harmless; she was dangerous to one of you."

"Miss Quarles!" Willis exclaimed.

"Miss Quarles," Mr. Potter repeated. "She knew who inspired the killing of Evelyn Dwight and she knew why it was done. Who was it, Bulow?"

Willis shook his head again.

"Where were you the night Miss Quarles was killed?"

"I was—" Willis looked at Ivy and his voice faded out.

"You came home about midnight, drenched from walking in the rain. Where had you been?"

"I crossed the street and walked in the park for a couple of hours. I never saw Miss Quarles. I wasn't near the zoo where the papers say she was killed. I walked around the reservoir, around and around."

"In the rain? For your health, I suppose."

"I kept seeing Lenny when he came out of the prison. He looked so—lost."

"Can't you see that's all it was?" Ivy asked Mr. Potter.

He continued to look at Willis. "Why did you destroy Jepson's painting of the chimney?"

"You know that, too? That damned chimney," Willis's voice was thick. "That's where Evelyn and I used to meet. She called it her bank." He made a queer sound of stifled laughter. "And it was, too. I'll pay for the picture. It just—I saw it and—I'll make full reparations to Jepson."

"And your reparations to Lenny?"

Willis looked at him haggardly. "Lenny understands."

"Willis doesn't know anything more," Ivy said. "Can't you tell that he doesn't know anything more?"

"Look at him," Mr. Potter said. "Look at him! Remember this, Bulow. If that mob gets Lenny, if it lays a hand on him, you're as guilty of his murder as if you'd killed him yourself, and I'll see you pay for it."

There was a quality in his voice that no one had ever heard in it before. Then he ran for the Volkswagen. The mob had drifted away now. The house still burned, sending up showers of sparks as timbers fell. Thank heaven, there was no wind.

When he got behind the wheel of the car Mr. Potter hesitated, in spite of his desperate haste. Somewhere else the mob would be collecting but he could not cope with them now, not until he had the information he needed, the proof that must exist somewhere. Anyhow, the State Police could handle mobs better than he.

Should he get hold of Lenny Horgan? No, better leave him at the Morison house. It was maddening to be wasting time on a hunch. He made up his mind at last and shot down to the lower level, along the highway out of town, down the narrow dirt road that wound between trees to the river and the old picnic grounds and the stone chimney that stood on a cement platform, where a picnic shack had once been, in the midst of charred ground.

He parked his car with the headlights turned on the chimney, which Evelyn had called her bank, and then, realizing how far lights could be seen on a dark night, he switched them off and took out a flashlight.

"I saw her putting that loose stone back into place," Miss Quarles had said. "I knew she was hiding something."

There was a chance, a slim chance, so slim a chance that his heart was cold at wasting time when every minute counted, when no safe wall stood now between Lenny Horgan and a mob.

He took one dismayed look at the size of the great chimney and then, setting the flashlight on the cement platform, he squatted down on his heels and began painstakingly to inch his way along, testing each stone, digging at it, pulling it, twisting it.

Fifteen minutes. He straightened up and began to work at a higher level. His nails were broken and his fingertips bruised and bleeding.

Twenty-five minutes. He had tried all the stones within easy reach on one side. Surely Evelyn wouldn't have used a ladder. He paused to consider the blackened smoke-stained interior of the fireplace but abandoned the idea. Not the dainty Evelyn, he thought. He began wearily on the other side.

Thirty-five minutes. He got up from his knees and started back along the line of stones at a higher level. He knew he had found the right stone the moment he touched it. It moved under his hand. He tried to pry it out and tore his nails. He used a pocket knife to dig at the putty, which crumbled into his hand. The stone fell forward so suddenly that it dropped on his foot.

For a moment Mr. Potter clung to the chimney, sick with pain. Then urgency became more important than the agony of the broken bone in his foot. He raised the flashlight and turned it on the space behind the stone, perhaps nine inches wide by four deep. He groped in it and pulled out a stack of currency, dollar bills, fives, tens, twenties. Evelyn's bank!

He thrust the money into his pocket and reached again into the space where the stone had been. There was an envelope. He opened it and pulled out a stiff piece of paper. For an incredulous moment he stared at it.

So that's it, he thought. That was the last thought he had.

Sixteen

The living room at the Tooling house was a huge room with a fireplace at either end, couches and easy chairs. As Willis and Ivy came in, they saw Claire bandaging Stan's hand, which he had burned while he was fighting the fire. Sylvia, who had sunk into a deep chair, was watching Claire with hard, implacable eyes.

"I wondered where you'd got to," Stan said.

"That man Potter got hold of me," Willis said.

Stan took a quick look at the other man's gray face, at Ivy who was clinging to his arm. His own face was haggard and streaked with soot.

"What became of Potter? Why didn't you bring him in with you?"

"He's gone."

"Where?"

"He said unless we can prove who murdered Helen Quarles the mob will get Lenny."

"And he thought he could prove it?"

"He's going to make a damned good try," Willis said with a short laugh.

Claire, who had been peering through one of the windows, gave a frightened cry.

"Stan! Those people are coming back! They are coming here. They must think Lenny is hiding at my house."

"Mix us some drinks, Willis, for God's sake," Stan said, "and then I'm going for the State Police. The phone is cut off and we've got to have protection."

He called sharply to Claire, "Stand back from the windows, darling!"

She felt for the switch and turned out the lights. "At least, they can't see us now and we can tell what is happening, what they are doing out there."

In the darkness, the fire at the Bulow house seemed to burn brighter. Now and then there was a crash of falling timbers and a shower of sparks. And always there was the roar of the fire itself.

"Stan, what are we going to do?" Claire demanded shrilly.

Outside, the mob had drifted back, a few at a time, quiet people who watched and waited. Here and there, a match blazed for a moment in the dark, the glow of a cigarette showed intermittently like a dull firefly. There were no words, no sounds. It would be better if they had made a noise. This patient waiting was more terrifying than violence.

Inside, they huddled in the darkness, trapped and helpless. Willis put glasses into their hands and they drank thankfully.

"That's better," Stan said. "Willis, can you manage alone?"

"I'll do my best."

"Don't let anyone in." He wheeled toward the window and paused, turned back, as there were exclamations, murmurs outside. A car had stopped. People were getting out.

They heard Morison's deep voice, shattering the stillness. "Go home where you belong! I'm ashamed of you. Decent citizens turning into a bloodthirsty mob. Go home, I say!"

"Thank God," Stan exclaimed, "Ross is with him. You won't have to tackle this alone. There's someone—I'll be damned. It's the Savage woman."

Claire, moving as jerkily as a mechanical doll that had been wound up, went to throw off bolts and chains, and admit Ed Morison, frail, shaking and indomitable, with Paula supporting him on one side and Ross on the other.

"Mr. Morison," Ivy exclaimed, "you shouldn't be out of bed."

"Try and tell him that," Ross said. "We've done our best." His "we" included Paula.

"I had to see for myself what was going on," Morison

said. "Don't fuss so. The people of Coxbury will listen to me. They always have."

"Where's Lenny?" Sylvia cried. "Ed, where did you leave Lenny?"

"He's in Florence's room. No one will look for him there. The very fact that the house is wide open will prevent them from searching it. Anyhow, there's not a man, woman or child in Coxbury who would attempt to storm my house."

When they had eased him into a chair, and Willis had brought him a drink, Ross explained how they had watched in horror from the lower level while the Bulow house burned.

"When I found a mob was gathering, I decided to see for myself what was going on," Morison declared. "I intend to have a part in whatever comes."

"I'm going out the back window," Stan said. "I'll get away down through that brook on the side of the hill. If I crouch over, they'll never see me. The brook is lined with big ferns and bushes the whole way."

"Be careful, Stan!" Claire called. "Be careful!"

"I will."

"And hurry!"

"All right. Don't worry. Close the window after me, Ross, will you?"

Stan climbed over the sill and let himself drop to the ground. "Okay," he whispered.

Ross closed and locked the window and went to join the others who had gathered around Ed Morison's chair, staring out into the darkness. Now and then a flashlight moved. There was a soft muttering sound now, the voices of people talking together in muffled tones. There seemed to be a great many more people than there had been, though it was impossible to guess their number, except when a flashlight suddenly illuminated white, staring faces, blank and dehumanized in that white light.

In the dark room, they waited helplessly, four women and three men, one of the latter incapacitated.

"If they weren't so terribly quiet," Ivy choked, "I could bear it better."

As though in answer to her comment a voice sang out, loud and demanding: "We want Lenny!"

At once, the mob took up the chant: "We want Lenny! We want Lenny!"

"O God," Sylvia moaned, "what have I done to my son?"

"Steady, there, Sylvia," Morison said in his deep voice, which was unexpectedly strong in spite of his obvious physical weakness. "You were never responsible for what happened to Lenny."

"Yes, I was responsible. I married Forrest. I gave Lenny a stepfather who always resented him."

"It's not fair to blame Dad," Claire said sharply. "Lenny was no good. He was never any good."

"Send him out!" The voice of the mob had changed, had swelled. "Send him out!"

"That mob," Sylvia said heavily, "is waiting outside to kill my son because they believe he's a homicidal maniac. They think he no sooner got out of prison than he killed Helen. But he didn't kill her. This can't go on. Not one more minute. Which of you killed Helen Quarles? You've got to tell the truth. Which of you?"

"We want Lenny!" The deep voices of men, shrill voices of women, a wilder note in them. "Send him out!"

"Which of you?" Sylvia repeated.

"Send him out!"

Like contrapuntal choirs, Paula thought. This is nightmare. That hysterical mob outside, and here in this room Sylvia Bulow, like the voice of fate, beating out her question. It's one of them, here in this dark room with me. One of them. And she had a curious repetition of the experience she had had with Miss Quarles. She smelled fear.

Behind her chair Ross's hands came down on her shoulders, drawing her gently back, and she leaned against him, comforted.

The mob had drawn nearer; shapeless blobs that were faces pressed against the windows, trying to peer into the darkened room.

"Willis," Claire cried in a panic, "we've got to get rid of them before they break in. I won't have this house trampled by a mob. All my lovely things——"

"We want Lenny! Send him out or we're coming in!"

A rock crashed through the glass. They moved farther back in the dark room until they were almost against the wall. There was no place else to retreat.

Claire started purposefully for the door. Ross dropped his hands from Paula's shoulders and seized her arm.

"Claire, what are you going to do?"

"Let me go!"

"What are you trying to put over now?"

"You're hurting me!"

"You don't get away from me until I know what you are up to. I don't trust you an inch, Claire. I never did."

"I'm going to tell them," Claire cried defiantly, "where Lenny is. It's our only chance. They'll kill us all. They'll spoil my beautiful house."

"You'd throw him to the wolves, would you?" Ross said, and his voice was queer. "You'd sell him down the river again! No, by God! Take one step toward that door, Claire, and you'll wish you were dead. For twenty years Stan and Willis and I have covered for you. Chivalrous little damned fools, that's what we were."

Voices were raised outside, conferring together, working out a campaign. Inside there was a moment's silence.

Then Claire said angrily, "Let go of me! You wouldn't dare act like this if Stan were here. You drunkard!"

"You asked for it, my girl," Ross said. "I'm telling you where you stand. One word to that mob and the truth about you will make a stench that——"

Ross gasped as she bit savagely into his hand and he released her. Like a flash she crossed the room, flung back the bolts and cried out into the darkness:

"If you want Lenny Horgan, he's hiding at Ed Morison's house in the housekeeper's room."

She slammed shut the door, pushed the bolt and turned to lean against the locked door. Ross switched on the lights and they stared at each other in silence.

Outside, the mob was drifting away, motors started, car lights moved across the lawn.

"Lenny," Sylvia cried. "O God. Lenny!"

"They won't touch him," Morison said reassuringly. "Believe me, Sylvia, they won't touch him. Not in my house."

Ross had not taken his eyes from Claire's face. "You always hated Lenny and you hated his mother. She was beautiful and you couldn't forgive that. He was brighter than you or your brother and he might inherit some of your father's money. You helped make life tough for him from the beginning.

"And then that summer Evelyn came along, and all of us boys fell for her. And you had fallen in love with Stan. You told Evelyn to lay off, that Stan was your property. You thought all you had to do was give orders and you could have what you wanted. And Evelyn laughed at you. She threatened to tell your father about Stan stealing cars; that would have ended him with Forrest. But good. I suppose she thought she could blackmail you as she blackmailed us. But you love money as much as she did. So—"

"I didn't kill her." Claire mouthed the words. "I didn't kill her."

"No, you didn't kill Evelyn. You invented the story Evelyn told Lenny, knowing he'd do anything to protect the mother he adored. You wanted to save Stan's nice position with Forrest, to keep him for yourself—

"You're like your father, Claire. You'd fight for what was yours, in spite of hell and high water. That's why you buttered up Helen Quarles all those years; you were scared as hell of her. You knew that if she ever talked, there would be a scandal that you couldn't live down."

"But what could she say?" Claire challenged him.

Ross watched her narrowly. "She could have said you warned her about Lenny; that you told her he was dangerous to her and she must never return if Lenny was freed."

Claire laughed.

"I think Evelyn told her about the lie you concocted about Sylvia and Mr. Morison. When Evelyn did anything she expected to be paid for it. She made a bargain with Helen Quarles. Don't tell what you know about me and I won't tell what I know about your dearest friend Sylvia."

Claire's breathing was uneven but again she laughed. "You think! You guess! You suspect! They're both dead. Prove it."

A car turned into the parking place.

"Thank God," Claire cried, "it's Stan with the State Police. I'll tell him how you have treated me. He'll—"

She put on the floodlights and slid the bolt. A small brown girl in slacks and sweater ran to the door.

"Who are you?" Claire demanded. "What do you want?"

"I am Molly Jepson. I must speak to Mr. Potter."

"Mr. Potter? He's not here. He left some time ago in a hurry."

"O God," Molly cried. "What shall I do? The mob has got Lenny Horgan! They are planning to lynch him. I've called the police but I've got to find Mr. Potter!"

She ran headlong toward the car, where a man with his head tied up in gauze was waiting for her. The car backed, turned, and went down the driveway.

Morison pulled himself to his feet. "We're going to the picnic shack," he said. "That's where they will take him. Those fools will listen to me." He added more firmly, "I know they will listen to me." He turned to the woman who still stood beside the door. "Come along, Claire."

"No," she said. "No!"

"On your feet," Morison said, "or Ross will carry you."

Seventeen

He had been buried alive. For a few moments of utter horror, as consciousness flooded back, Mr. Potter was sure of it. His nostrils and mouth seemed to be clogged with something that shut out the air. His cheek grazed against gritty earth. Earth? It was soot he smelled.

Had he been knocked out and locked in the burning Bulow house? No, there was no fire. But there was soot, soot in his nostrils, in his mouth, against his cheek.

His arms were pinned to his side and he could not move them. He tried to free his wrists. He was not tied, he was wedged somewhere.

His head throbbed, he was dizzy for lack of air, lancing pain from his right foot hurt him unbearably. He moved it and blacked out momentarily from agony. He moved the left foot, kicking downward and heard soot drop onto concrete. Concrete? He had been knocked out and wedged into the stone chimney!

At least, he hadn't been buried. But how long, he wondered, would he remain conscious without more air than he could get through his soot-clogged nostrils and mouth? He tried to shout and no sound came out. He swallowed soot, and tried to spit it out.

Suppose someone started a fire in the great chimney? Don't think of that, he warned himself grimly. Someone would come. Someone was bound to come. Captain Foote would look for him, and O'Toole and the Jepsons. Someone was bound to find him, someone had to find him. Because now he knew the answer.

But Captain Foote, he remembered, was busy organizing men to protect Lenny Horgan. He had a mob to deal with. And if the mob reached Lenny first—but they wouldn't find him at Morison's house. They wouldn't search Morison's house. He was safe. He had to be safe.

I've got to get out, Mr. Potter thought desperately. Once more, he tried to dislodge himself but he was too tightly wedged. He could not budge his arms. He dared not move his right foot. From the grating feeling that had caused such excruciating agony he assumed that he had broken a bone. All he could do was to kick with the left.

But what was the idea in putting him up here? Would he be left to die? Did the killer think he would not be found—or that it would not matter if his body was found? Or was it simply panic and an instinctive play for time?

There were muffled voices somewhere but he could not make out where they were or who they were, and it mattered terribly who they were now that he knew who had killed Helen Quarles and why.

From below he heard Molly cry, "No. I won't go back. I'm a better shot than you are."

"We can't hold them alone, Molly. Don't be an infernal idiot."

"We have the revolver."

"But a girl with a revolver and a man with a concussion can't hold back a mob. You'll be hurt."

"We can't go away. We've got to do our best."

"Okay," Kurt said. "You're right, of course, but I wish to God I'd never laid eyes on Hiram Potter."

For all this uncomplimentary reference, Mr. Potter was exultant. He tried to speak and could not. He kicked out with his left foot and heard loosened soot and cinders fall below.

Molly cried, "Kurt! Kurt! There's something up the chimney."

"Stand out of the way there." In a moment a flashlight beam crept like a finger up the chimney.

Kurt shouted, "Good God, it's Potter!"

Again he moved his foot, dislodging cinders.

Then his feet were grasped and jerked. As the broken pieces of bone in his right foot grated together he fainted. When he opened his eyes it was to hear someone groaning. The sounds were coming from his own big mouth, he thought in shame, and stifled them.

He lay on the cement platform, his hair and clothes covered with soot and ashes. While Molly was wiping out his mouth and pouring brandy into it, he choked and spat, drank again and tried to sit up. Beside him, Kurt, weaving on his feet, held a flashlight.

"What the hell were you doing up there?" Kurt said coldly.

"Having fun," Mr. Potter said faintly. "Thank God, you found me."

"Hiram," Molly steadied him with an arm around him. She looked in despair from his face, blackened beyond recognition, to Kurt, white faced and dizzy.

"We've got to hurry," she cried. "Oh, Hiram, they've got Lenny!"

"Who has?"

"The mob! They are coming here to lynch him. That's why Kurt and I came. We couldn't find you and we had to stop them somehow."

Mr. Potter looked from the groggy man with the bandaged head to the small girl and smiled faintly. "We'll stop them."

He tried to get up and subsided with a groan. "Damn it, I can't put any weight on my foot. I've broken something."

There were car lights streaming across the picnic grounds, the slam of doors, a muffled roar of voices. The mob was pouring across the flat ground. In front, two men dragged a helpless man between them up to the cement platform.

From the other direction, converging on the chimney, came a small troop of people, headed most improbably by Morison.

Stan ran toward them, his jacket half torn off. "I called the State Police. They're coming. I had an awful time reaching them."

As the men in front, dragging Lenny, approached the platform, three people stood facing them. They must, Mr. Potter thought, be the most ridiculous sight ever to face a ravening mob bent on death. In the middle stood Molly, five feet of determination, a revolver in her small hand. On her right Kurt stood weaving, his bandage hanging rakishly over one eye, clinging to Molly's shoulder to hold himself upright. On her left, Mr. Potter, face and fair hair black with soot, coat ripped and covered with ashes, hung on to her other shoulder because he could not put his weight on his right foot. He wondered grimly how long the slim girl could uphold the two staggering men.

He took the revolver out of Molly's hand.

"Stop! I'll shoot the first man who comes one step further."

He looked over the heads of the approaching mob. Sister Ann, Sister Ann, do you see anyone coming? But there was no police car on the road. For a bad moment he thought the men would rush him, particularly an ugly fellow with a great coil of rope in his arms.

"All I ask," Mr. Potter shouted, "is time to speak my piece. You've got hold of the wrong person and I'll prove it to your full satisfaction if you will be fair enough to let me speak. Ten minutes. That's little enough, isn't it? Ten minutes?"

"He's stalling for time," someone yelled warningly.

"Look at me," Mr. Potter said. "The killer of Helen Quarles jammed me up that chimney a few minutes ago to keep me quiet. If you think I'm in an easygoing mood—"

Surprised, baffled, the mob hesitated. Without momentum a mob loses its frenzy. When its madness is gone it ceases to be a mob, it separates into its component parts, it becomes men and women again.

"Ten minutes," Mr. Potter said, his voice hardly raised above a conversational tone, because the mob had become so still. "I'll give you the facts. You can draw your own conclusions. But don't go through the rest of your lives knowing you've murdered an innocent man. Lenny Horgan doesn't even know who killed Helen Quarles but I do. That's the story I want to tell you now."

Unexpectedly Morison's big voice boomed from behind him. "Give the man a chance!"

"This is the story," Mr. Potter said, "of four boys and two girls. Most of you have known the four boys all their lives: Ross Bentwick, Stanley Tooling, Willis Bulow and Lenny Horgan. They were, in a most unusual sense, devoted and loyal friends. Of the two girls, one was Claire Bulow, now Mrs. Tooling; the other was Evelyn Dwight, a juvenile delinquent if I ever heard of one, and a flourishing blackmailer."

Mr. Potter's voice was easy and conversational; his eyes still remained fixed on the highway along which the State Police cars should be coming. His audience, he was well aware, was too keyed up, too geared for violent action, to listen long to his quiet words. He had to startle them, grasp their attention.

"How good a blackmailer she was," he went on, raising his voice a trifle, "is proved by the money I have just found in her cache here at the chimney, which she called her bank. And with good reason."

Still clinging to Molly's shoulder he put his other hand in his pocket and pulled out the great handful of currency. He waved it at the crowd.

There were exclamations, excited murmurs. Their eyes fastened on it.

"I had better," Mr. Potter said with a friendly grin to the mob, "get rid of this before I am tempted." He turned to hold it out to Morison. "Sorry I can't move," he apologized. "I think I've got a broken foot."

With an exclamation, Ross moved to the front of the platform and took most of Mr. Potter's weight on his arm. "I hope to God you know what you are doing," he muttered.

"Sometimes," Mr. Potter said in a low tone, "you have to take a chance, and this is the only chance Lenny has —unless we want to see him dangling from a rope on at chimney."

He looked down at the three men who stood at the dge of the platform, two of them strangely uncertain, the third watching him, white faced yet with a forlorn sort of hope. Ross began to talk fast in the rumbling undertone which with most men passes for a whisper.

"Well," Mr. Potter went on, "as everyone knows, Lenny Horgan killed Evelyn Dwight. But there was one mighty queer thing about the case. He never said why he did. When he stood in the dock on trial for his life he made no defense of any kind; he offered no explanation. He confessed his guilt and took his punishment—twenty years in the penitentiary.

"And that is where Miss Quarles becomes important. She saw the murder done and, being an honest woman and a good citizen, she gave the evidence that convicted Lenny. But she was unhappy about that evidence. Why?"

He paused only a moment. "She was unhappy because she had discovered something that upset her terribly. She had discovered a piece of evidence that showed someone else had a powerful motive for wanting Evelyn to die. Later, when Evelyn had been killed and Lenny offered no reason for his crime, Miss Quarles suspected why he had killed her. But she wasn't sure. And since Lenny was guilty, she kept silent. Anyhow, I think she realized the situation had gotten out of control. Lenny hadn't been intended to kill the girl, just to scare the everlasting daylight out of her."

The crowd was quiet now; he had their attention. But the hold on Lenny's arms had not loosened; the man with the rope still held it coiled between his big hands.

"So long as Miss Quarles stayed abroad," Mr. Potter went on, "the person who was morally responsible for Evelyn's murder felt safe. But she must not be allowed to return home. There was, somewhere, a piece of evidence that she must never be permitted to find. Every year, as most of you know, her cottage has been ransacked in search of that piece of evidence."

He paused while the murmuring grew louder, while heads nodded, while startled speculation grew in the eyes that were becoming less those of a mob than those of responsible men and women.

"Oddly enough, and as a kind of wry justice, the net result of that constant searching was that the cottage could no longer be rented and therefore Miss Quarles was forced to come home to live in it. For years she had been warned that Lenny would be revenged on her for her testimony against him if he were ever freed. But when there was no more money, she had no choice. She came home.

"With her return, the danger arose that she would break down and tell the truth to her dear friend, Sylvia Bulow, whose son's life she had helped to destroy. So Miss Quarles had to be killed. But Miss Quarles, on the day of her death, had a long interview with Mrs. Savage who was coming to work with Mr. Morison. She told her that she was in danger from Lenny Horgan. While Mrs. Savage was still with her, Miss Quarles had a telephone call. She explained to her caller that she had told Mrs. Savage everything. That night someone broke into Mrs. Savage's apartment to get a look at her so that she could be recognized later. The following morning, someone tried to push her in front of a taxi. So she came to tell me about it."

He looked along the highway but no cars moved on it. He looked down at the mob who watched him, silently now. Behind him he was aware of the people who stood motionless. At his side Molly still tried to prop up her shaky husband, and Ross stood holding his weight on his arm. The pain in his broken foot was growing unendurable. The mob before him blacked out, came clear again, slanted at strange angles. It would be too humiliating to faint like a Victorian heroine.

Mr. Potter tightened his grasp on Ross's arm and drew a long breath.

"Well," he beamed at the waiting faces confidentially, "you begin to see my problem. I came up here to look around. First, I found out why Lenny had killed the girl. He had been told a lie, a particularly filthy lie, which concerned his mother's relationship with Mr. Morison. I don't hesitate to mention this pathetic secret, which Hor-

gan kept so valiantly and at such a tragic cost to himself
for twenty years, because there is not one of you, knowing the principals, who will not know that it was baseless.
But he was only a kid, only sixteen, and he adored his
mother. He believed his stepfather was capable of killing
her. He wanted to protect her.

"And because his motive was based on a lie, I wondered who had evolved that lie. So I looked around and
I discovered a funny thing. There wasn't one of his
friends who did not have a real motive for wanting Evelyn Dwight out of the way. There was his friend, Ross
Bentwick, for instance. There was his stepbrother, Willis
Bulow. There was Stanley Tooling. All of them trapped
by Evelyn, all of them fearing exposure.

"Now all of these boys, men now, knew or suspected,
as time went on, that Lenny Horgan had been victimized,
but they remained silent. Even tonight, when you had
turned yourselves into a mob, a vicious mob; when Ross
Bentwick had nearly lost his life because you had tampered with his car; when the Tooling car had its tires
slashed; when the Bulow house had its windows broken
and then was burned to the ground; even then they remained silent. Why?

"Ross Bentwick once said he had begun to drink because he couldn't endure knowing he was a chivalrous
heel. Queer words, aren't they? Were all of them chivalrous heels?

"So we come to the other girl in the picture."

In the distance there was a car with a red blinker on
its roof, and Mr. Potter expelled a little sigh of relief.

"We come to Claire Bulow Tooling, who hated Lenny
and was jealous of his mother. Claire, who is the only
one of the lot capable of concocting that filthy lie about
Lenny's mother. Claire, who wanted Evelyn driven away
from Coxbury."

"Stop him, Stan," Claire cried. "He can't be permitted
to say things like that about me."

"Wanted her dead—" Mr. Potter's voice rose.

The police car had stopped behind the mob and men were piling out of it.

"Wanted her dead," Mr. Potter went on relentlessly, "because Evelyn was having an affair with Stan Tooling whom Claire had marked as her private property; wanted her dead because Evelyn had it in her power to destroy Stan's nice position with her father; wanted her dead because Claire wanted the money as well as the man."

O'Toole, Captain Foote and two State Troopers, trim in their smart uniforms, were forcing their way through the crowd, revolvers drawn. The two men who were holding Lenny released his arms. The man in front let the coil of rope drop with a thud on the ground.

The detectives were coming up on the platform now.

"No!" Claire cried. "I didn't kill Miss Quarles. It was Stan. He did it for me. She was dangerous to me. She'd have told them—she knew from Evelyn I'd made up that story about Sylvia. Mr. Morison could have driven me out of town, out of my beautiful house. She was dangerous to me."

The detectives were on the platform now. "What the hell are you doing, Potter?" Foote whispered.

"Claire Tooling—" Mr. Potter's voice carried to the last person in the mob.

"I didn't," she cried. "I didn't! I telephoned Miss Quarles but I didn't see her. Stan advised me not to. He said he'd cancel the appointment. But he went out that night. He went out. Only he did it for me. He did it for me."

"He did it for himself," Mr. Potter said. He nodded to O'Toole. "Stanley Tooling killed Miss Quarles; he tried to get Mrs. Savage run over; later, he drugged her at his own party with sleeping pills he had stolen from his sister-in-law. He gave Mr. Jepson here a concussion when he searched the Quarles cottage last night. Thirty minutes ago, he knocked me out and stuck me up in the chimney."

He sighed. "You might search him, though he probably destroyed that paper I found in Evelyn's cache." He added, "Not that it matters. You'll find proof when you need it."

"Where, for God's sake?" O'Toole muttered desperately.

"South Carolina. Twenty years ago, before he knew he could get Claire Bulow, Stanley Tooling married Evelyn Dwight. I had the marriage license in my hands a few minutes ago. Not legal, of course, because he was under age, but if Claire had found out—"

O'Toole laid his hand on Stan Tooling's arm.

Stan turned blindly from face to face. "Claire?" he said. "Claire?"

She jerked away from him, her face hard. "You were married to her! But I thought you were protecting me. You've made a fool of me. I'll never forgive you for that."

She turned away and walked alone off the platform, alone across the picnic grounds, alone up the highway toward her beautiful house.

Stan swayed as O'Toole snapped handcuffs on his wrist and led him through the silent mob toward the police car.

And then, unexpectedly, Lenny called, "Wait, Stan! I'm going with you." He managed a diffident smile. "After all, I know the ropes."

Eighteen

Captain Foote sank wearily into the chair Morison had indicated. He had had no sleep and he showed it, though he had taken time to shave. For a moment he sat looking from face to face. Unexpectedly, he chuckled.

"What," Mr. Potter asked mildly, "do you find so amusing?"

"You." Captain Foote shook his head. He made a gesture around the room. "You. Here's a nice quiet little rural community and you come into it. Three days! And look at you. You've got a broken foot; Jepson has a broken head; Lenny Horgan has broken ribs and he's all banged up; Mr. Morison has a heart attack; the Bulow house has been burned to the ground; the Toolings have their tires slashed and their windows broken; Bentwick's car has been demolished; Mrs. Savage has been drugged; Jepson's painting has been slashed to pieces."

Molly nodded. "I've always told Hiram that he has all the domestic virtues of the man-eating shark."

"But at least," Jepson consoled her, "he does make things happen."

Mr. Potter threw up his hands in surrender.

"When you people have had your fun at Mr. Potter's expense," Sylvia said, "I'd like to try to find some words, however feeble and inadequate they may be, to express my gratitude. Last night, he saved my son's life and made it possible for Lenny to live here, to re-establish himself, to begin all over again."

Mr. Potter flushed a trifle but he grinned at her. "What saved Lenny," he said, "was the quixotic action of the Jepsons who came here alone to face a mob. What re-established Lenny was his loyalty and his magnificent generosity when he knew Stan had killed Miss Quarles, and his determination to stand by in his defense when he himself had so nearly been lynched by the mob for her murder."

"Stan stood by me the best he could," Lenny said in his quiet voice. "I don't think you understand him. He's an easy-going guy and he wanted things nice for me. He wanted them nice for everyone."

"Especially," Mr. Potter said dryly, "for himself."

"Well, he'd been awfully poor, you know," Lenny said apologetically, "and then my stepfather took a fancy to him and he saw he could have a nicer future than he had ever dreamed of. When he realized he could get Claire, he knew he'd be secure for life. Stan's the kind of guy who has to be secure. I can understand how terrified he must have been that Claire would find out he'd been tricked into that marriage with Evelyn. Claire wouldn't like that, she'd never forgive that. She'd know he had lied to her all along."

Mr. Potter looked from Ross to Willis. "When you two got to thinking about it, you knew Claire had prompted Evelyn's killing didn't you? And you protected her, Willis because she was his sister, and you, Bentwick, because—"

"Well, we couldn't help Lenny then. He'd actually done the killing. And to betray Claire would be to spoil her life and Stan's. The only thing was that I couldn't go to see Lenny. I knew if I did, it would break down my resolution."

"Who did you think had killed Miss Quarles?" Mr. Potter looked from Willis to Ross. "Never mind, you don't need to answer." He smiled faintly. "Obviously, you both had a low opinion of Claire."

"Not after the Quarles cottage was ransacked," Ross said. "I saw Stan there and I couldn't figure it. By that time I didn't know whether Claire or Stan was behind the Quarles murder. But when I knew of the attacks on Paula I got rid of all my boyhood loyalties in a hurry. I was through with standing by."

"I assume," Mr. Potter said, "Claire won't help her husband."

Ross laughed shortly. "What do you think? She tries to get rid of Evelyn who, all the time, was Stan's wife. She'll never forgive that. Never."

Willis said angrily, "She is arranging to sail for Europe as soon as she can and she is going to put her house here in Coxbury on the market. She'll have to come back for Stan's trial, of course, but she'll never help. It will be her testimony that will send him to the chair. I'll—do what I can for the guy."

"It seems to me," Mr. Potter said mildly, "you take a rather casual attitude toward murder."

"Not casual," Ross said. "Never casual. But I've said before and I'll say again that there are worse things. Stan broke poor Miss Quarles's neck. Well, God knows he will pay for that. But Claire—who incited Evelyn's murder—who was the reason for the Quarles murder, because Stan would never have killed her if he could have trusted his wife's loyalty—Claire made those murders possible, made them inevitable. And she is within the law. You can't put feelings on trial."

"I suppose," Mr. Potter said thoughtfully, "Stan lit out from his house last night as soon as Ross told him I was trying to find Miss Quarles's murderer before the mob got Lenny. He must have realized I was on the track of that cache of Evelyn's. So he knocked me out, pushed me up the chimney, and then set off calmly to get the State Police. The thing I can't figure out is how Miss Quarles was ever persuaded to go to that meeting in the park."

"That was Claire," Willis said. "She told me this morning. She's doing all she can to make sure Stan is convicted. Now that the whole community knows what she is, she has to punish someone for that. She's made that way."

"While all the rest of you," Mr. Potter commented, "have to punish yourselves. Odd, isn't it?"

Willis nodded. "Well, anyhow, Claire called Miss Quarles who told her about talking with Mrs. Savage. So she arranged to meet her and find out what Mrs. Savage knew. When she told Stan what she had done, he advised against it and said he would break the appointment for her to save her leaving the house. The phone was shut off to keep reporters away. So when Claire heard of the murder she suspected Stan had killed the woman. She was scared as hell but she thought he had done it because Helen was dangerous to her."

Mr. Potter shook his head. "There's only one person who has been dangerous to any of you from the beginning." He looked from face to face. "Yourselves. You hated Evelyn and you wanted her dead. And when she died you had to punish yourselves. Willis became repressed to the danger point; Ross tried to turn himself into a drunk; Claire tried to make herself invincible; Stan tried to find safety; Mrs. Bulow turned to food for compensation. It's time, isn't it, for you to forgive yourselves?"

He grinned at them. "Personally, I think it is high time you all got out of prison."

"That's good advice," Morison said. He sat very erect in the chair behind his desk. This morning, for a man who had suffered a heart attack, he looked surprisingly well. He glared at his nephew, trying in vain to conceal his deep affection and his pride.

"I suppose you know," he said grimly, "that you've acted like a damned fool. You had me figuring you were involved in this whole sorry business." He held out his hand and Ross clasped it.

He grinned at the old man. "Damned if a little excitement doesn't seem to be good for you, Uncle Ed!"

Morison grinned back. "I gave that mob hell," he said in a tone of satisfaction. "Sent them away with their tails between their legs. What with nearly lynching the wrong man, and Lenny behaving as he did, they're a sick bunch of pups right now.

"I told them while they were trying to overthrow the law and murder a man in cold blood without trial or any chance to defend himself they were unfit to live in a democratic country.

"I told them it's law that took man out of chaos and made him a man and not an animal; and when they destroy that, when they let their hates and their fears master them, they're unfit for civilization; they'd better go back in the trees for a couple of centuries before they are ready to come down and walk the earth like free men.

"I told them—"

He grinned reminiscently. "A sick lot of pups," he repeated. "When I get to work on my book on Coxbury I'll not mince words in saying what I think of them." He glanced at Paula. "I don't know how you feel about going on with this work—"

"Well—" she hesitated.

Mr. Potter broke in. "I was talking to Graham Collinge yesterday. He thought I was running a port of missing actors up here. He said you and Bentwick would make a terrific team."

"That's an idea that has been growing on me," Ross said. "How about it, Paula?" He smiled impudently. "This is one scene I could play better without an audience."

"Run along," his uncle told him. "But when you have kissed your girl come back here. We have things to discuss." He turned to Lenny. "I've got a job open for a collaborator. Would you care to try it?" He added sternly, "Put down that chocolate, Sylvia. You're going to start reducing. I expect you to lose forty pounds this year."

Willis straightened his shoulders. "I've got to get down to New York and arrange for a defense for Stan." There was a new decision in his voice. "Coming, Ivy?"

"Wherever you say, darling."

"I'm more sorry than I can say," Willis told Kurt, "about that painting. Something just blew up all of a sudden. I'll mail you a check today. The worst of it is that the painting was good. Better than good. I'd like to talk to you about doing a portrait of my wife. When—things are more settled I'll write you about it."

Mr. Potter collected the Jepsons and Captain Foote with a glance. Sylvia stopped them before they reached the door.

"Mr. Potter," she said very quietly, "that was good advice you gave us about getting out of prison. But haven't you overlooked something?"

"What is that?"

"Your own private prison. You've been in it for a long time, haven't you?"

For a moment he seemed on the verge of retreat into his own separate loneliness. Unexpectedly he smiled. "Much too long," he admitted. "I'll have to do something about that."

"The best chiller of the year!"
—*Cosmopolitan*

BURNT OFFERINGS

A novel by
ROBERT MARASCO

WHEN MARIAN ROLFE FOUND THE LISTING IN
THE WANT ADS, IT SEEMED ALMOST TOO GOOD TO
BE TRUE:

> *Unique summer home. Restful, secluded.
> Perfect for large family. Pool, private
> beach, dock. Long season. Very reason-
> able for the right people.*

AND THE ROLFES WERE THE RIGHT PEOPLE.
MARIAN KNEW IT THE SECOND SHE FELT HERSELF
SURROUNDED BY THE AUBUSSONS AND CRYSTAL.
AS FOR BEN, HIS DOUBTS ABOUT SOME "CATCH"
SEEMED SILLY. UNTIL, STEP BY STEP, THE HOUSE
AND GROUNDS BEGAN TO EXERT THEIR POWER AND
PLUNGE THE ROLFES INTO A NIGHTMARE OF
EXQUISITELY MOUNTING HORROR.

*"BURNT OFFERINGS terrifies. Even by day-
light it makes your flesh crawl."*

—*New York Times*

A DELL BOOK $1.50

If you cannot obtain copies of this title from your local bookseller, just send
the price (plus 25¢ per copy for handling and postage) to Dell Books, Post
Office Box 1000, Pinebrook, N. J. 07058.

BESTSELLERS
FROM DELL

fiction

- [ ] **THE TAKING OF PELHAM ONE TWO THREE**
  by John Godey **$1.75**
- [ ] **EVENING IN BYZANTIUM** by Irwin Shaw **$1.75**
- [ ] **THE MATLOCK PAPER** by Robert Ludlum **$1.75**
- [ ] **BURNT OFFERINGS** by Robert Marasco **$1.50**
- [ ] **ELLIE** by Herbert Kastle **$1.50**
- [ ] **ELEPHANTS CAN REMEMBER** by Agatha Christie.. **$1.25**
- [ ] **DUST ON THE SEA** by Edward L. Beach **$1.75**
- [ ] **PEOPLE WILL ALWAYS BE KIND** by Wilfrid Sheed **$1.50**
- [ ] **SHOOT** by Douglas Fairbairn **$1.50**
- [ ] **THE MORNING AFTER** by Jack B. Weiner **$1.50**

non-fiction

- [ ] **LOVE AND WILL** by Rollo May **$1.75**
- [ ] **AN UNTOLD STORY** by Elliott Roosevelt and
  James Brough **$1.75**
- [ ] **THE WATER IS WIDE** by Pat Conroy **$1.50**
- [ ] **THE BOSTON POLICE DIET AND WEIGHT CONTROL**
  PROGRAM by Sam S. Berman, M.D. **$1.25**
- [ ] **QUEEN VICTORIA** by Cecil Woodham-Smith **$1.75**
- [ ] **GOING DOWN WITH JANIS** by Peggy Caserta and
  Dan Knapp **$1.50**
- [ ] **TARGET BLUE** by Robert Daley **$1.75**
- [ ] **SOLDIER** by Anthony B. Herbert **$1.75**
- [ ] **MEAT ON THE HOOF** by Gary Shaw **$1.50**
- [ ] **THE LEGEND OF BRUCE LEE** by Alex Ben Block ... **$1.25**

Buy them at your local bookstore or use this handy coupon for ordering:

| Dell | **DELL BOOKS**
P.O. BOX 1000, PINEBROOK, N.J. 07058 |

Please send me the books I have checked above. I am enclosing $_____
(please add 25¢ per copy to cover postage and handling). Send check or
money order—no cash or C.O.D.'s. Please allow three weeks for delivery.

Mr/Mrs/Miss_____

Address_____

City_____ State/Zip_____

This offer expires 7/75